tomorrow's jackpot, ha, with the [

Henri asked if he had children.

'A son. Very ill.'

'Sorry. What's the matter with him?'

'Adolescence, that's what. No terminal disease, for better or worse.'

Henri sneezed.

A year ago, he too had driven taxis. Had he been a pest himself? No. More of the Zen type, minding his own business. He had always posited that hairdressers, masseurs and the like would be better recipients for confidences than a man behind a wheel.

Only bicycles would make him go ballistic. Insolent cockroaches that multiplied exponentially.

The inevitable happened: road-rage drove him to topple one over deliberately. As bad luck would have it, the rider was an off-duty policeman. In short, he lost both taxi and driving licence.

'… taxes! Tell me about it! Do you know that I hardly pocket forty percent of any fare after insurance, petrol, what have you, and goddamn syndicate fees?'

Henri did. He also knew about the recently launched Renault sporting coupé, President Giscard d'Estaing's philandering, and whatever mesmerised people these days. What he was interested in, right now, were scented mimosas, the flowers akin to yellow snowflakes.

'Monsieur, you are obviously not familiar with the place. They don't grow by the sea. But yes, they are in full blossom at this time of the year. Go inland. That's what I do. On my own. To be alone is an undervalued luxury. Some claim that it takes two to be happy. Why? What are they afraid of?'

His voice become mellow, its intonation dreamy, Henri felt like asking him for a beer. There was something endearing about the man.

But that would not have fitted his new character. Besides, they had arrived in front of the Negresco Hotel.

'Here's my card, young man. Do not hesitate to call. Be careful. People around here smell a sucker a mile against the wind. And hookers tend to dress as divas,' he added with asthmatic emphasis. 'Beware…'

The improbable philosopher skittered away.

Henri held on to his crocodile briefcase, recalling Count Sàndor's admonitions a few days ago. 'You are henceforth my private secretary of noble descent. Rule number one: never look astonished. Display neither zeal nor contrariety. Two: move and talk slowly – nonchalance, my boy, is quintessential. Three: no over-tipping. Vulgar. Four: whatever your request or complaint, address them to directors or owners only – in other words, not to subalterns – employees if you will. Then … yes: no explanations, no justifications, regardless of circumstance. *Qui s'excuse s'accuse*. Fundamental: be polite. Always. Last not least: do not, unless absolutely necessary, pay cash. A well-bred gentleman normally doesn't carry any.'

Two doormen, clad in eighteenth-century livery, wig and all, rushed to get his luggage.

To think that, not so long ago, these tasks were incumbent on him, wearing T-shirts and, in winter, anoraks!

He looked up at the Negresco's famous pink dome towering over the Art Deco façade. Henri had seen pictures in various travel guides or magazines, but here was a postcard come alive.

His awe was cut short by some important-looking man

who scurried to greet him and whisk him into the hall. There again, he gaped, mesmerised by the massive crystal chandelier commissioned by Czar Nicholas II and never delivered due to the Revolution – but Henri remembered not to look impressed. Wearing sunglasses helped.

Formalities were swift. His passport? 'Not necessary, sir. Your credentials precede you,' the director mellifluously smiled. 'So sorry that our august Madame Augier cannot greet you in person.'

He was shown into a junior suite. Junior! Twice as big as what he called home in Paris, a dump on the fifth floor of a dilapidated house without a lift.

Having unpacked his brand-new wardrobe, he strolled out of the hotel, waving aside the solicitude of a staff paid to lavish it.

It was a mild month of February. White and navy-blue tents lined the beach in front of the hotel, reminiscent of Thomas Mann's Venetian Lido.

Henri smoked and reflected. He hadn't been granted all this privilege in exchange for nothing. 'To sing for one's supper' came to mind, but most certainly would have made the Count scold him. Be it as it may: time for a change of clothes and dinner in the hotel's reputed Chantecler restaurant, whose Gobelin tapestries and rococo furniture he'd observe with a suitably blasé gaze.

The place was practically empty and the maître d' more than willing to engage in conversation – especially with someone ordering the best Chablis to accompany lobster on scallop mousse.

Henri had hinted that he was Count Esterhaffy's distant nephew. This elicited frenetic fuss. Superlatives reverberated all around the dining room; the average age of the personnel close to geriatric, they remembered the old aristocrat vividly.

'*Cher maestro* – if I may call you so,' murmured Henri, lighting a Montecristo at the risk of choking, 'Count Sàndor has asked me to look up a relative of ours, Valentine. Her last name? Don't know for certain. Possibly married more than once. Anyway, she's fortyish and bears our family mark: jade eyes. She married at this hotel two years ago, on Saint Valentine's Day. The Count, now too weak to travel, learnt about it in the society columns. Could you possibly help?'

Granted, Henri thought, my approach isn't all too subtle, but no shortcuts are.

The maître d' scratched what remained of his hair.

'The eyes, yes. Absolutely. Became some princess or other by marriage, and would not let you forget it. Mind if I sit down? My hip's killing me. The calvados is on the palace…'

Henri waved a magnanimous hand toward a chair.

Half a bottle later, the maître d' turned loquacious.

'Her eyes, *oui oui*. But one mostly saw her teeth. Always laughing, even the day a dog was almost run over a few feet away. Might I express my opinion?'

'Please do,' retorted Henri.

'Nice yet totally stupid. Talked non-stop, droning out clichés. Only months after the wedding the Prince fled to Monte Carlo. With displeasure, as he held that farcical pirate state in contempt. However, if I again may venture, anything was better than the brainless drivel he had to endure from the dumb blonde with the big boobs!'

'Where might Valentine be now?' asked Henri, eager to cut to the chase.

'She'll be here on the 14th. Believe you me. When you have no convictions, you revert to superstition. This said … I myself have given up reading the headlines. Too depressing. I cut straight to the horoscope.'

Another unexpected philosopher.

'Name's Monsieur Gaston, by the way. At your service, sir. As to Princess Valentine, she'll be hunting for a new husband. What better place than this?' he added with a gesture embracing his humble self.

Having regained his quarters, its linen sheets and down pillows, Henri called Count Sàndor. Not much to report, other than his illegitimate offspring would probably appear five days later. The kind of information required from him. Problem: how reliable was it?

He then had the television removed. Hated the things.

In its place, a huge bouquet was delicately deposed. Is this how gigolos live? Or was it the stuff of fairy tales? If so, he had no children to tell it to and never would, for he also hated children.

His mind rewound to the conversation that had led to this surreal situation, only weeks before.

***

'As a taxi driver, you must have heard captivating stories, some indecorous. Do listen to mine. I have a daughter. When I saw the coverage of her wedding to some decadent prince, I might as well have looked into a mirror. She is the replica of my features, from the aquiline nose and voluntary chin, the slender fingers to, of course, the jade eyes. Her legs are a bit askew, just like mine. Now…I know for certain I'm the girl's father. But I do not know who the mother is. Original, is it not?'

Quite. It was usually the other way around.

'Exactly,' resumed the Count. 'I led a very agitated life. God only knows how many children I produced in the process.'

Here he threw his hands heavenwards.

'God should never have rested on the seventh day of creation. He overslept the concept of justice … and relegated us to a waiting room, unsure as what we're waiting for. God-ot, uh? Sorry. Digressing. Where was I? Yes. Valentine is my child. Does it really matter? What does, is to find her. As I'm much too old and far too obese to travel anymore, would you, perhaps…?'

He collapsed, thus unable to finish his sentence.

The waiters in their by now familiar café rushed to take the old man's pulse. Beating, albeit feebly. An ambulance arrived. Henri fought hard to be allowed to sit by his friend's stretcher.

He spent the night holding his hand.

At dawn, emerging from his near-coma, Count Sàndor asked him to dial a number.

An hour or so later, a man in black barged into the room. He uttered inscrutable words, offered a complicated handshake, and looked like an undertaker. Turned out he was a lawyer.

The Count, reading his thoughts, mumbled that the two professions were not altogether different. Aware of impeding surgery, he made it snappy.

'I want Henri Durand to be given full flowers, sorry, powers over my Monaco account. He is to pose as my secretary and relative in Nice. He is to be treated as such at the Negresco. He is to locate my daughter Valentine. It's my last wish – other than many gargantuan meals sprinkled by the best Romanée-Conti, naturally.'

It looked as if Count Sàndor had stopped breathing. Not so. Malicious eyes darted at him, then at the sinister lawyer.

'Write. "I, Count Sàndor Esterhaffy, hereby…"'

On February 1st, Henri received a sealed envelope containing an Amex platinum credit card, a sum of cash the like of which he'd never seen before, and a confirmation from the Negresco Hotel for an unlimited stay. The note was laconic. 'Not prone to outpourings, I thank you for your assistance. It confirms my instinctive trust in you, Henri. Sàndor E.'

***

Dazzling events had succeeded one another at a dizzying pace. All of them due to the domino effect of coincidences – random chance events, if you will – that had led to his encounter with the aristocrat.

Had he not, one day, been hailed by a short but handsome man who turned out to be Jean d'Ormesson; had the illustrious writer not appreciated his good manners to such an extent that he subsequently hired him as his private taxi; had they not been stuck in a colossal traffic-jam and started talking – no way that he, Henri, would, in February 1980, be pampered in one of Europe's most legendary hotels.

Encouraged to do so, he had told d'Ormesson about his passion for travel books. Especially classic guides, such as 1913's Bradshaw, the Murray and Baedeker, the Appleton or the Guide Bleu collections.

Violating his vow of silence, so to speak, Henri had further opened up about his childhood. His father had been a driver of tourist buses criss-crossing Europe. He would return starry-eyed. The contrasts! The learning! The people!

His mother had been a supermarket cashier. Treated with benevolent disdain at best, with rude impatience most of the time, her daily life was a constant source of frustration she unleashed unto her husband, making home a living hell. She was jealous of his happiness. Also furious that her son would listen to him as though he'd been a year-round Santa Claus, his stories lavish presents. Roaming around with the proverbial rolling pin, she'd slam it around and scream.

Aggression reached such proportions that Henri's father had, one rather uneventful evening, diverted a knife from the salami he was slicing to slit the shrew's throat. He then redirected it towards his own and repeated the exercise.

Henri, fast asleep whilst this double deed was committed, was fifteen years old and later entrusted to his aunt's care, clearly his mother's clone in terms of charm.

'Marriage has not precisely represented an idyllic state of affairs since then.'

Jean d'Ormesson, allergic to melodrama, had been amused by Henri's narrative.

'Do you have friends?'

'Books. Books are my only friends.'

Upon alighting, the writer's tone became authoritative.

'Tomorrow morning you will drive me to the Quai Conti. At eleven sharp. Wear ironed trousers and a long-sleeved shirt. Understood?'

Almost opposite Notre-Dame, the Quai Conti was in walking distance from where the illustrious man lived. So what? He'd probably be asked to wait for hours, but with the meter ticking...

In front of the impressive façade of the Académie Française, the following day:

'I have a surprise for you, my friend,' d'Ormesson beamed with those limpid blue eyes whose capacity for wonderment was notorious. 'Park on the sidewalk. Do as I say. I brought a jacket and a tie. You know how to knot a tie, don't you?'

The writer was greeted with the reverence due to his eminence. Well – Henri did know that the French Academy had been founded by Cardinal Richelieu under Louis XIII. Still. However: that the pomp had survived drastically-changed circumstances was intimidating.

'I shall leave you in the library for a few hours as I must fight for the first woman to be elected (wink). Normally these premises are strictly off-limits to non-members. Enjoy it to the full.'

Other than the gardens and vast salons, Henri discovered that M. d'Ormesson, with many acclaimed works to his name, had become one of the forty 'Immortals' – as they had called the privileged few since times ... immemorial. (The only member ever forced to resign had been Marshal Pétain in 1945, for obvious reasons.)

Later, asked about his impressions, Henri uttered not a word: nothing was so apt as to describe that trance.

He heard nothing from d'Ormesson for a long while.

During that long while he lost his taxi and driving licence, due to the incident already mentioned. Shit bicycles.

Great was his surprise, one evening, upon hearing the following message on his answering machine. 'This is Jean d'O. Miss your loyal services but am cloistered on Corsica to write in peace. I forgot you not. There is a library called Mazarine, also created by a Cardinal, near the Academie.

It's normally reserved to university students etc. Well. As they have recently acquired classical travel books and guides, I took the liberty to inscribe you as my pupil. *A bientôt.*'

***

Devoid of resources, Henri spent his days at the Mazarine. It was heated, it was lit – saving the *centimes* he counted to pay for electricity. And so beautiful! Wood-panelled walls; high ceilings crammed with books; dimmed chandeliers and green-shaded reading lamps. As an old-fashioned bibliothèque would look in Wonderland.

This is where he met Count Sàndor.

As antiquated as the surroundings, he was always dressed to the nines, arriving with a cape and a fedora, wearing a bushy moustache, a rimmed monocle and some flower in his lapel.

Henri, who had adopted the discipline of wearing ironed trousers and shirts, oftentimes felt observed by the old – and very, very fat – gentleman.

One evening, a thunderstorm broke out moments before the closing hour. As violent as unexpected, it drew the two men under the awning of the nearby café.

'Shall we go inside and have a sherry?'

'Er, well, with pleasure,' stuttered Henri, 'but I forgot my wallet and…'

'No problem. May I introduce myself? Count Sàndor Esterhaffy.'

Hands shaken, they sat at a corner table thankfully half-circled by a banquette, for the Count's monumental frame could hardly have fitted into a chair.

'You intrigue me, young man. Forgive my bluntness. I never had patience for banalities.'

His heavy accent and husky voice fitted the silhouette. Retrieving a silver cutter, he went through the motions a cigar connoisseur would.

'Are you an inveterate traveller?'

Henri blushed. Admit he was as poor as a church mouse and had never gone anywhere beyond Northern France, only a few hundred kilometres away? By train in order to save petrol, with a student ID some pimpled guy had forgotten on the back seat of his taxi?

'Thought so,' the old Count kindly smiled.

'What about you, sir?'

'Ah. On January 1st I shall be ninety on the dot! Meaning I was born in 1890. In Hungary. We travelled by horse-carriage or on horseback, then. My family owned, well, land, castles, racetracks, vineyards, whole hills in the Carpathians ... all taken away. First by bandits, including family members and imperial ministers, then by the communists.'

Despite a hint of nostalgia, his voice, devoid of bitterness, sounded bemused.

'In any case, travel I did indeed. I married seven times,' he chuckled.

'But wasn't yours a Catholic country? I mean in Italy, divorce was only legalised in the...'

'Right. But in Hungary, everything is different. Must be the folklore, the mix of traditions, the volatile temperament... Our past mingles all the ingredients of sagas – turmoil, chivalry, treason, romance, and so forth. Read about it, will you? Lucidity blinds the old. Novice minds, as children's eyes, are often the wisest!'

They chit-chatted about the chance factor in life. They joked about pride and prejudice. They drank more than one sherry.

Next day, Henri, the first to arrive at the library, immersed himself in all the books he could find about Hungary. It was daunting to comprehend all the territorial and regime changes. Discouraged, he concentrated on the history of families such as the old man's.

He learnt that the Esterhaffy had been made 'perpetual counts' in the fifteenth century, when Magyar culture was at its zenith and Latin the cohesive language of noblemen – a symbol of independence against German expansion. Until 1848, a turbulent year in *Mitteleuropa*. Noblemen were exempted from taxation but obliged to fulfil military duties at their own expense. Hence the proliferation of small armies and fortresses. The Kingdom's crown passed from one lineage to another in a rather haphazard fashion. Dynastic or political alliances through marriage or other stratagems, aside from all-out war, proliferated; feuds between Transylvania, Slavonia, the Palatine, the Capetian House of Anjou and…

To hell with it. Henri skipped most of that.

What did arrest his attention was the conversion of many Orthodox landowners to Catholicism in the sixteenth century. Aha. But then Lutheranism and Calvinism spread under the Catholic Habsburgs. Confusing. In any case, the communist leader Béla Kun had, after World War I, abolished all titles and ranks whilst nationalising aristocratic estates. This had been ratified again in 1947, this time by the Soviets, who vandalised and confiscated what little was left of the nobility's property.

So: was Count Sàndor no Count after all?

The latter walked in. Observing Henri's perplexity in front of piled-up books, he smiled with bonhomie.

'May I invite you for another sherry at our café?'

The young man nodded humbly.

This particular evening was diaphanous. They sat down on the terrace, glancing at the Louvre and the *bateaux-mouches* gliding by.

'You are handsome, as you surely know. A haircut wouldn't harm. Has any resemblance struck you?'

'Who with?'

'Me.'

Henri looked up. Had he been too gauche to lock glances with the count the day before? He saw it now: very pale green eyes.

'We could be related,' the aristocrat remarked. 'Can you imagine that I had, once upon a time, black hair like yours? That I was as slim and sprightly?'

Henri kept silent. He was no liar – not yet.

'Yes, I was handsome too. It helped. You see, in my youth, one travelled from estate to estate presenting nothing but a visiting card and one's appearance as an introduction. Major-domos were to assess the acceptability of both. If satisfied, you were *persona grata*, thus offered hospitality. Sometimes overnight; sometimes for weeks or months on end. Imagine this, nowadays!'

The Count's constant jangling his key ring was enervating. Still, Henri asked what happened next.

'Everything, my friend. The war. Actually, two of them. In between, a facetious upholding of tradition, meaning, for the likes of us, of semi-normality. But with the Russian occupation, the Old Order atomised for good. Exile, dislocation … call it what you will. A Nansen passport, for the better connected of us. My brothers had died, one of typhus, the other lethally wounded. My parents had fled to Portugal, courtesy of some distant Bourbon cousins.'

Henri's exhaustion dwindled. He felt as if he were listening to a storyteller in front of a fireplace.

'In love with a French lady, I and my butler mounted an old motorcycle, he in uniform, me wearing a black tie. We drove through devastated landscapes and roads swarming with caravans of refugees. Once in Paris, I sold my last gold coins which allowed us to share a room in a *pension* and buy some clothes. We shared three pairs of shoes, fortunately taking the same size.'

Count Sàndor lit another cigar. Today, Henri observed him with emotion. The delicate care with which the ritual was executed did suggest times of deprivation.

'And then?' he softly asked.

'Oh. Then.'

Following the curl of the smoke with an ambivalent expression, he coughed. A bad cough.

'Henri. How can you understand? In those post-war years, we aristocrats had all lost a lot. Most of us anyway. But here in Paris, my name opened doors. The embassies. The Radzivills. The Rothschilds. Louise de Vilmorin, herself just divorced from a cousin of mine and surrounded by the, back then, litteratis and glitteratis. Jean Cocteau, St Exupéry, Matisse, the Coopers, what have you. Like everyone else, I fancied her.'

'Was she the one who had prompted you to come to Paris?'

'Certainly not!' protested Count Sàndor. 'Louise was a witty bitch oozing charm but washed with all waters. No. The object of my devotion was a young lady of provincial provenance, pretty in an innocent way. Not too luminous in the upper compartment, but so very kind. One night, I bring her back home on my motorcycle and get stopped by the police. No papers whatsoever. I had believed in my lucky star. A mistake. I am incarcerated. The young lady is taken home. She tells her parents she's in love with an exiled Hungarian who is presently in jail, has not a penny, whose servant pays for their room thanks to the tips given to a butler at receptions and who, during the day, roams the streets pushing a cart with a discordant bell he's stolen somewhere, sharpening knives.'

Henri, for the first time in a long time, burst out laughing. He could picture the destitute nobleman criss-crossing the better *quartiers* of town, peddling his trade, possibly wearing a top hat and impeccably attired, notwithstanding frayed collars and cuffs.

'Funny?' grumbled the Count. 'Her parents didn't think so. They removed Sophie to some remote Aeolian island, and that was that.'

'How did you overcome this … er…?'

'Last sherry, shall we?'

Henri's head was spinning. But he couldn't well ask for food, could he? Count Sàndor summoned the waiter.

'Two more glasses and a steak tartare for the gentleman, please.'

Without transition:

'Thanks to another woman, my friend, how else? I was fluent in four languages. Other than my eyes, my Oxbridge English mesmerised the American actress who would become my second wife. Next stop: Hollywood. The most vulgar place I've ever seen, but, in the circumstances, the most comfortable. Fascinating too, for there were the likes of David Niven, Clark Gable, Gary Cooper, Greta Garbo and company … heavily resculptured, most of them, but would I see them without make-up? Unlikely, as my ferociously possessive wife scanned life with the sharpest of radars. Didn't prevent her from dying in a helicopter crash.'

'Oh my God! So sor…'

'God had nothing to do with it, as Mae West would scoff when someone goggled her jewellery. Point being, I was wealthy again – and free! Amongst other things, from the servility so often engendered by gratitude. Anyway. Having dutifully played the widower, I bought a flat in New York where, years later and money dwindling, I'd become Ella's domestic stallion. I was handsomely rewarded, allowing me to book a suite at the Brenner's in Baden-Baden in the summer, another at the Negresco in Nice in the winter. Two of the most elegant hotels in those yesteryears!'

He threw a self-depreciating glance at Henri.

'She, ironically, would be left by two of her six husbands for one and the same woman – carnivorous but beguiling Louise.'

Henri fiddled with his fork. Intimacy made him uneasy.

'Let it be said that I meant well and made women happy. As to Ella, she collected husbands, titled or lacking that, obscenely rich. Oh! Stop looking like a shrinking violet. Besides, do tell, my young friend: wouldn't you like to dispose of a small fortune? Supposing fortunes can ever be called small?'

Some question!

***

It was now February 10th and Henri had spent a whole day in bed, wallowing in what he had never known: idle luxury.

After a long bath and a chapter of *Motoring Through France*, Edith Wharton's early-twentieth-century account of an automobile trip (she's now in Saint-Rémy de Provence), he determined: Nice's nightlife, here I come. He insisted upon the hotel limousine: again, an employee might provide precious information pertaining to Valentine.

The chauffeur was about his age. First annoyed (older men have more knowledge) then enchanted (as the guy looked cheeky) he distractedly mentioned (aloof tone):

'I want to have fun. To spend money. Some pretty and not too shy a girl. What do you say?'

'Leave it to Sebastian, say I.'

He lowered the tinted window separating the front from the back seat, whereupon a sort of hydraulic system was activated, presenting Henri with a well-equipped mini-bar, frosted glasses, and a tray of canapés.

That's the life, chuckled the ex-taxi driver who only two weeks before had been chasing mice in his attic.

Opening the car door, Sebastian announced:

'Le Palais de la Mediterranée on the Baie des Anges. Once the city's most grandiose such establishment. All you want is inside.'

Henri tried not to look puzzled.

'A casino, sir. Need I say more?'

Henri strolled in, hands in his pockets.

The muffled commotion took him by surprise. The surroundings were splendid – not so the people. Henri had imagined a strict dress code; instead, he observed open shirts, sneakers and the like. He zigzagged, unfamiliar with roulette, blackjack or baccarat tables. Formally dressed as he was, he found himself harpooned by some hostess offering him a pink drink he thought wise to decline. Moments later she returned with a bottle of Krug. The idea, other than cajoling him into parting from loads of cash? Obvious.

He noticed towering chips of various colours in front of certain players. Thousands? Millions? Palpable tension suggested stakes were high. He'd ask Sebastian.

The good-humoured chauffeur greeted him with a warm smile.

'Thought so. Not your scene. Right?'

Henri, feigning to resent the familiarity, glided back into the limousine with dignity.

'No other casinos in town?'

'In French or in Italian?'

'Meaning?'

'Well, sir, the word casino in Italian has an altogether ... different meaning.'

'Such as?'

'A *bordel*. A whorehouse, if you prefer.'

Henri readjusted his tie and activated the system presenting him with trays.

'Sir. There is another gambling casino in town. Should you be interested. Mostly thronged by Italians.'

'The Mafia?'

'If you must call a black cat grey, yes.'

'All right, let's go. My experience of gambling dates to my voyages to Uruguay and Hungary,' Henri lied.

He was getting the drift of it. Lying, embodying a man he was not, adopting postures and turns of phrases unfamiliar to him, required improvisation. It amused him. His father's teasing advice? 'In order to seduce a woman, best not to be yourself.'

'Sebastian, put me into the picture, will you?'

'You look on a mission. Journalist?'

'No. A spy.'

'Do such pitches sell?'

The chauffeur snorted. It was his lucky night. A cretin if he ever met one. Or what in French you call *un pigeon*.

The Ruhl casino was everything Sebastian had suggested – and worse. Count Sàndor would have been appalled. Black-and-white photographs on the wall. Monochrome furniture. Beigeish carpets. Everything reminded one of porridge. Even the chairs and sofas were covered with lava-coloured leather. Nowadays' idea of taste? Soon homes, with surfaces only meant to unwrap catered food, would be decorated in such a fashion. The age of instant coffee and screens replacing paintings on the walls was dawning. Had there been books (an absurd hypothesis) they'd have been bought by the metre. Or else ordered by weight.

Henri walked around, then out.

Noticing his sombre mood and good at taking his client's mental temperature, Sebastian reverted to a cheerful voice.

'To lift your spirits, sir. La Chunga in Cannes. The prettiest girls. Excellent food and schmooze music. Live.'

'Okay – I mean, excellent. Allow me to invite you.'

'But sir, I couldn't possibly…'

'Yes you can. You're a rogue.'

'But…'

'No buts. I need to ask you a few questions.'

At three in the morning, having drunk himself into an ethylic stupor, Sebastian had said more than he would remember the next day.

Henri learnt that he and Valentine had had an affair.

That the limousine driver only liked daft women was not the bonus: that she spent money as if there were no tomorrow was. A broken clock shows the right time twice a day. Yes yes, a well-known saw.

On the way back to the Negresco (Henri driving) his drunken companion slurred out a few details Count Sàndor would be interested in: Valentine defined her mother as 'a serial seducer without sentiment whose atrophied heart amputated men and women alike'.

'Sorry? Isn't that a bit brainy for a brainless…'

Sebastian was snoring away. Henri parked the limousine round various corners from the Negresco.

Back in his junior, ha, suite, he reread his father's last letter. Had he already opted for death?

My son.
The other day, waiting for some trivial repair to my bus in a gloomy garage, I read a magazine called – forgot what. In any case I learnt a word. I transcribe: 'Palimpsest, from *palimpsestus*, meaning "scraped clean and ready to be used again"'. The Ancient Greeks used wax-coated tablets to write on with a stylus, then erased the writing by smoothing the surface and write again. Isn't that what life is all about? It seems to me that we draw over the same patterns ad infinitum (that expression I happen to know!). May you be different from your mother, a frustrated person, and from me, a romantic with unfocused desires and no goals other than bus itineraries. Identify malice. It's a sneaky form of evil. You can and you will, my son. <u>I'm proud of you already</u>. Not of myself, explaining why I no longer love life.

It was tantamount to exerting pressure. Explaining,

perhaps, why Henri had never dared fall in love, or strive for achievement. He'd never live up to those lofty expectations. The stakes set too high, he'd always feel inadequate.

Jean d'Ormesson's one-time remark surfaced into his mind: 'Depression is nothing but chronic self-pessimism. You have to be happy to become lucky. It requires discipline.'

Discipline? How could it be mustered in the absence of authority or a mentor (same thing?). Henri's thoughts drifted to increasingly bleak places. How often had he pictured his pop idol, Claude François, throwing a hairdryer into his bathtub? What had triggered his death wish? He'd accumulated fame, fortune, sexy fans… Had the unconditional love of a father drowned his self-esteem early on? Henri would look it up in some library or other.

The insistent ringing of the telephone ejected Henri from his rueful ruminations.

'Sebastian here. Back among the living. What do you say to an excursion? Free of charge. With a stopover. At a cousin of mine. A surprise. Also a solution.'

To what, exactly? Henri agreed and slept on, until, at seven in the evening, attired *petit marquis* style, he settled in the limousine.

Sebastian: no cap, no uniform. He rolled up the separating screen without a word.

They arrived in a small village perched above the Riviera's corniche, vaguely familiar because of the movie *To Catch a Thief* with Cary Grant and Grace Kelly. Roquebrune.

A jovial character in his fifties flung his arms around Sebastian. After much shoulder-slapping, he turned to Henri.

'I hear you saved my cousin's life or at least his job last

night by driving without a licence.'

'But… how do you know?'

'I'm an ex-police officer just as you're an ex-taxi driver.'

He bade them into his house.

'Ready. Stamp and all. Only thing I need is a photograph and a name. What about a pastis, to start with?'

Christ, thought Henri. Pastis. The modern substitute for absinthe, especially when undiluted, and Sebastian's cousin didn't look the diluting kind. What was this all about?

'You're getting a new driving licence, man,' Sebastian casually informed him. 'Forged but valid. Now. Better change your name.'

An hour later, Henri Durand was holding a document which not only allowed him to drive but also to call himself Heinrich Esterhaffy – Count Sàndor's nephew or perhaps son, he hadn't decided yet.

Quick and simple! Who doesn't like that?

Money? 'No way,' the cousin cheered, more backslapping at hand. 'Please leave as my better half is about to come back from some church or other, unaware of my, er, hobbies.'

Sebastian asked Henri to sit in the front. Henri refused. He needed to reflect. Things were getting on one hand easier, on the other trickier. You start with a small lie and then the domino effect kicks in.

Suddenly, the Monte Carlo casino.

Another postcard! Dazzled, he stepped out of the car, taking in the spectacle. Built in the mid-nineteenth century, it must have had a serious facelift, as it looked coated in meringue with starch on top. The fluorescent illumination pimped up the kitsch.

Henri let himself be spun through the revolving door.

'We need chips. Do you have cash?'

Aha, Henri realised, alcoholic haze notwithstanding. Yet he did as told, meaning handing over a bunch of banknotes in exchange for plastic rectangles. Sebastian would not pocket any.

'Let's boogie. Allow me to teach you a thing or two. There are tricks. Some based on rigorous mathematics.'

He let himself be dragged to the roulette table.

'Do observe attentively.'

Henri must have looked the novice that he was.

'Casinos are legal crooks. Croupiers are experts. Even the most dexterous of them cannot determine the winning number. However. Throwing the ball in a certain way, they can avoid it falling into a given zone. Of course, the numbers they try to avoid are those on which the biggest stakes have been laid. This is why you must always play against the biggest betters. Do not drink. Never let a girl be thrown into your lap. Both diversions would drive you to be reckless. Also, avoid the oldest trick in the book: pushing a chip onto the winning number with an imperceptible movement of the shoulder. Assuming only your hands are under scrutiny. It used to work. No longer. As to baccarat: some casinos excel at manipulating cards, whilst shuffling them. It's called "slicing a sausage".'

The now officially fake Count understood precisely nothing. Besides, Sebastian's staccato elocution got on his nerves.

Yet Henri was not the cretin he endeavoured to look like. Only hours later, he and Sebastian, acting as total strangers, were accepted into the exclusive, private rooms.

They would place chips on all the numbers ranging from nineteen to thirty-six. Simultaneously and discreetly, Henri would toss an equivalent sum on the *manque* square representing numbers inferior to eighteen. The idea? Simple: whatever the winning number, the result is nil and, whilst Henri would lament his loss, Sebastian pocketed the gains, there being far too many people around the table for the croupiers to remember who played what. As to the cashier, he displayed no astonishment at seeing Henri time and again exchanging ever greater sums for chips. Indifference had become his second nature.

Though elated, Henri realises it's time to go.

'But it's only three o'clock,' protests Sebastian.

'Let's have a drink at the Hotel de Paris.'

***

This mollifies his mentor in the swindle business. Henri ends up driving back to Nice. Same procedure as the previous night, except for being the proud holder of a fake driving licence. He leaves a third of the casino cash in the glove compartment and strolls into the Negresco. An evening well 'spent' warrants a rest more than 'earned'.

This once, Henri dreams blissfully. He dreams of the happiest moments of his childhood when his father took him to the gardens of the Champs Elysées. There – other than the stamp market – were the puppet shows. The boy never tired of trying to figure out how the strings were pulled, or how voices could flow out of rag throats. Gradually, he mastered the art of a ventriloquist.

Upon emerging from his late-morning haze, Henri laughs.

We were now three days from V day.

High time to gather more useful information.

Unavoidable Sebastian was waiting in the hall when Henri walked down the spiralling stairs. In his uniform, and bowing:

'Good morning to you, sir.'

'What brings you here?' Henri belched with an irritation Count Sàndor had expressly censured.

'The Princess. The lady you are obviously keen on meeting. Arrives today. I am to fetch her from the airport. Her first stop, Hermès. Should you happen to, er, find yourself there, you could, possibly. You know.'

Could the guy not formulate sentences without chopping them up? But this was no time for semantic subtleties.

'By the way. Pleased upon opening the glove compartment this morning! Thanks.'

Mercifully the rogue had not inherited his cousin's propensity for backslapping.

Henri, weary of the hotel's refined atmosphere and not a little pleased thinking of the huge amount of cash locked in his safe, sauntered to the market in the old town. What a joy to walk by makeshift seafood stalls where aproned men shucked oysters! To savour them on a bed of ice with chopped shallots, fresh lemon, bread and Normandy butter on some zinc counter, with local wine in a *pichet*!

Valuable information indeed! Pictures of Valentine, a living replica of the Count, wearing a black veil more fitting to a widow than to a fresh divorcee, were spread all over the local papers. She was due that very day and would, 'for sentimental reasons', stay at the Negresco Palace.

The ball had started rolling. Sebastian had left a message at the hotel's desk.

'She's dining at the Opera restaurant. NB!'

To hell with the Hermès shop. Henri changed yet again

– pretending to be rich required enormous amounts of clothes and energy – and reserved a table.

Walking into the restaurant, she spotted him at once. Henri, let's not forget, was strikingly handsome.

Picking at her food, she waited. In vain. 'Let her make the first move,' Henri had determined.

Some tiresome pseudo-gypsies created the pretext.

Valentine waved in his direction.

'Would you mind sitting at my table? Might you tell these people to stop their racket?'

With a polite grimace of reluctance, Henri did.

Here we skip half an hour of introductions and small talk, before realising, what a coincidence, they stayed at the same hotel. Both on the fifth floor.

'What brings you here?' Henri inquired.

'Valentine's Day. My first name happens to be Valentine.'

'Is that so? Born on a February 14th perchance?'

'How perspicacious!'

The maître d' at the Chantecler had been right about big boobs.

'You look at everything with the attention one devotes to things we wish we'd share with an absent person.'

She added, her teeth on full display:

'Something I read in a book on the plane. I threw it away – the book, of course. Drivel. A sentence such as my mother collects. She's a narcissist, see?'

This statement was uttered with the pride of a pupil who learnt a new word.

'She might be playing a role,' Henri ventured, conciliatory.

'She's done nothing but. Married five times. Playing a part grants one a place in life.'

'Where did you read that?' Henri teased.

'Same book. In the bin. Are you stupid or what?'

After a pause allowing her bosom to heave, she purred:

'Tomorrow I'll allow you to take me to the beach.'

Thinking of Count Sàndor, Henri responded that he would be enchanted. Nothing further from the truth. That girl was for sale and he, no toy boy. In jeans and without make-up, she'd be quite plain. And then, the Swiss accent!

They walked back to the Negresco. Henri suddenly longed for the television to be brought back. What would lonely, not to mention old, people do without it

With a fluted voice meant to sound sophisticated, Valentine suggested a nightcap at the hotel's bar.

'Sorry beautiful, but I must make a phone-call. To America. Business.'

'Oh! Where to?'

'New York.'

'Really?' she exclaimed enthusiastically. 'My mother used to live there!'

'Is that so? Please tell me all about it tomorrow. Shall we say eleven in the hall?'

'Twelve. Never before twelve.'

The connection was bad and the Count not sounding too well either.

'I found your daughter. Charming, of course.'

'*Très spirituel.* What did you find out about her mother?'

'Other than she lived in New York at some point, not much. I promised Valentine lunch on the beach tomorrow. Should know more next time I call.'

'Good boy.'

The line went dead. A surge of adrenalin fuelled a sudden idea, made him call Sebastian.

'I'll make it short. That cousin of yours. Might he be of more... assistance?'

'Yes.'

'When?'

'Anytime.'

'Like tomorrow at six?'

'Sure.'

'See you then.'

'No problem.'

The good thing about the man: no about turns. On the other hand ... there was something radioactive about him.

Valentine was wearing the kind of hat you wear at the Prix de l'Arc de Triomphe or Ascot, totally out of place on a drizzling February day in Nice. Her outfit matched.

They looked like a cocotte and her pet as they stepped into the beach restaurant. Embarrassing. Valentine paraded. She had booked in her name – of course not her maiden name – meaning she was greeted with bows and much 'Her Highness' toodeloo. Graciously, she waved all the homage away, insisting all she wanted was a small table and simple food.

What he needed was to make her talk. Being the talkative kind, she would. Flattery was the key.

'I'm sure your mother isn't remotely as beautiful as you are,' he started.

Valentine shrugged demurely, then asked:

'Are you rich?'

'No.'

'Too bad.'

'Sad too.'

'Never mind. What's your last name, Henri?'

'Does it matter?'

'Depends.'

'Would a title be of importance?'

'I already have one. Best thing about the whole hard work. I'm a big snob, see?'

Another person you didn't have to decipher the subtext with. Henri began to find her quite amusing after all.

'Do tell more.'

'Daahrlink, much to tell. But there are many blanks – the whitest one being I do not know who my father is. Many possible ones. Mother says that a woman without a man is like a fish without a bicycle.'

This elicited much mirth. On her part.

'Were you never tempted to find out?'

'…?'

'Who your father is?'

'Oh. That. Not really. I was brought up by two, my mother's Texan husband and my mother's lover. I bear no remote resemblance to either, and rather liked both.'

Was she as candid as she pretended to be? According to the Count, she must have been about forty-two. Had she always been blonde, or merely reached the age when most females' best friends are their hairdressers?

Chit-chat ensued, which Henri steered towards faraway countries. Valentine having roamed many; he, read about them, their globetrotting bantering turned out to be entertaining. Her view was that museums and sightseeing were far less telling about a culture than shopping – that's where you met local people. And the people she had most enjoyed meeting weren't the ones ransacking the Vuitton shops dotted all over the map, but the ones you met in street markets, antique bazaars or groceries.

Henri closed his eyes.

'Mother of course never came with me. While she paid guides to show me monuments, I bribed them to take me to more fun places,' she chuckled.

Awoken from daydreaming, he remembered his mission.

'Tell me more about your mother.'

'Ask me no questions, I'll tell you no lies,' Valentine chirped. 'I shall love you all the more if I'm afraid to hurt you.'

What? But all right; if she wanted riddles, he'd repay in kind.

'I see her as you imagine yourself.'

'Irresistible, eccentric, or both?'

'Certainly not inexpensive,' grumbled Henri with a disarming smile.

She had ordered a double tray of seafood composed of crayfish, lobsters and what not. Simple food indeed. Obviously not disinclined to gulp down Château Minuty with largesse, the bill was extravagant.

Having cast an oblique glance at his credit card (on which Count Sàndor's name was embossed) and at his cuffs (with the family's emblem on them), Valentine had drawn hasty conclusions. Noble and shy. She particularly valued the latter. Too many ladykillers around. Take that sexy chauffeur, Sebastian. A pure product of greed. (Valentine had no more such trivial worries, having taken her ex-husband, the Prince, to the cleaners.)

She was intrigued by his offhandedness. Insecurity feeds infatuation. Meanwhile, Henri thought there was something disquieting about her. She was everything and its obverse.

As they walked back to the hotel, she kept silent. Most peaceful.

'You're not the flirtatious kind, are you?'

'No,' admitted Henri.

'Married? Homosexual? Mourning...'

He swivelled round, removed her sunglasses and, emphasising every syllable, said:

'Lady. None-of-the-above. A-lo-ner. *Voilà.*'

Valentine recoiled. Had he been brutal?

She, about to nest her cheek against his shoulder and he, about to stroke it, a strident exclamation made both of them jump.

'My sweet, sweetest heart! There you are! And in such handsome company! I'm overjoyed! Come kiss your mother dearest! I wanted to surprise you for Valentine's Day! Let me squeeze you, my little lamb!'

Why didn't the bombastic redhead call her innocent too while she was at it? Valentine became white as cocaine.

They were both trailed into the bar.

'Tea or cocktails? Who cares? Young man, put me in the picture!'

The verbal deluge that followed allowed no such thing. Esteemed Baroness Tresch, as the obsequious waiter called her, never drew breath until she announced she needed a siesta.

Valentine and Henri found themselves face to face again.

'You wanted to know? Here goes: husbands, preferably Hungarian, and horses, always thoroughbreds, sum up her life. The first allow Mother to buy the second, until she loses at the races. Her presence here indicates she's broke again.'

Henri did not invite her to his suite. Nor did he call the old man, even though both thoughts hovered in his mind.

***

The next day was February 14th. The breakfast room was festooned with heart-shaped balloons.

Henri, gathering that ladies slept late, arrived early. Miscalculation. A perky Valentine slithered to his table no sooner had he ordered.

'I slipped Mother some pills. Mixed with Alka-Seltzer, she'll never be awake before late afternoon.'

Such was her glee that Henri didn't show irritation.

'Here's the idea, dear Count-whatever-you're-called: let's have fun. Just you and I.'

This reminded Henri of his rendezvous with Sebastian's cousin later that afternoon. Cancel it?

'C'mon! I know a place where they sell disguises. Let's buy wigs, hats with holes, and stuff. Let's pretend to be poor – really poor. I've spent my life dolled up. Oh please!'

She looked lovely and frothed with excitement.

'My name, today, will be … whatever you decide.'

'Bonnie – call me Clyde, honey pie.'

She imitated his drawl.

'Swell. Let's laugh all the way away from the bank, yeah?'

'Sure thing, cheeky chick.'

By noon, Henri didn't look like the taxi driver he was, or had been (it was a bit blurred as they had already drunk a whole lot of wine) but like an authentic tramp. Valentine, in rags and tatters, plus the wig, looked like some Cleopatra miscast in *Les Misérables*. His ventriloquist gifts served him well. Other than limping like a hunched old beggar, his quavering elocution compounded by hardly moving lips intrigued passers-by. His imitating French slang made her roar with laughter.

Henri? Had he not, perchance, met Count Sàndor on a rainy day outside a library, he might well be neither faking poverty, nor with a frivolous but attaching woman. Less still, shuttling between Nice and Monte Carlo in limousines or, for that matter, hanging out with thugs in casinos.

How could he possibly prolong this scam?

By lying, of course.

To the authorities, no dilemma: he'd go through with his identity theft. Kleptocracy had given him more than enough reasons for retaliation. But double-crossing his benefactor?

When does a minor lie turn into high treason?

'Oh God,' Henri whined.

'Sorry?' Valentine chuckled as more coins were dropped in the basket they had placed in front of them. 'God?'

'A figment of … guilt. Infused by an absentee landlord.'

As someone laid flowers at their feet, Henri hissed:

'Enough is enough.'

'Let's have a really good lunch then! Hey! This is my special day!'

Henri dragged her to an alley, peeled off his white beard and other accessories, told her to do likewise, but she refused. Typically, she had had left her clothes in the shop. No make-up remover either.

'Weirder like that!' she exclaimed. 'Smart-looking guy takes a low-life to a fancy restaurant. Let's see what happens.'

They returned to the Opera. It was the best.

Its owner, a charming lady in her seventies, threw them an incisive glance without batting an eyelid.

'I imagine you smoke. Let me prepare a table on the terrace.'

'Interesting,' whispered Valentine. 'From the way I look she pictures me with a fag dangling at the corner of my mouth. Let's see if she brings wine with one glass only, presuming I drink from the bottle...'

The food was exquisite.

'Don't worry about the expense,' said Valentine. 'And stop looking like a shrinking violet.'

Hadn't Count Sàndor used these very words? Atavism.

'What's wrong with pretending to be someone you aren't? We simply put on a disguise. Nothing to write home about! Think of all the fakes and frauds in the world. Take ... well, take Lola Montez, the Bavarian King Ludwig's some number or other mistress. Lola was Irish, called Miss Oliver I think, not a drop of Spanish blood in her veins. Mata Hari was completely Dutch, her real name Margaretha can't remember what...'

Margreet Zelle, Henri did not interject.

'... anyway. Exotic? C'mon. Other than the first lived in India for a while and the second in the Dutch Indies...'

'Now Indonesia.'

'... nothing wrong with imaginary identities!'

She laughed. He cringed. Had she unmasked him?

'I know how elegant you are, dear, but honestly! Don't be more Catholic than the Pope! Yes, I know, we should not have accepted the coins thrown into our lap but hey, they were only coins. Lighten up, my charming Count!'

A close one. Just to divert Valentine's attention, he pointed out that the poet and novelist George Eliot was in fact a woman called Mary Anne Evans, who had chosen a masculine pen name in the belief she'd be taken more seriously, and as to George Sand...waste of time. Valentine had long ceased to listen.

36

She removed her ugly dentures, her gloves, her wig, and handed the flabbergasted owner a bundle of banknotes. Way above the bill's amount.

'You couldn't have been kinder,' she beamed, displaying her white teeth made in America. 'We shall be back, shan't we, daaaarhling Henri?'

The restaurant's owner darted an icy glance.

Henri was glad he hadn't cancelled his expedition with Sebastian. How to get rid of Valentine? Well. Lying. Again.

'I have a secret errand to run,' he murmured in such a way she immediately suspected he'd slip off to buy her a present.

They parted ways in the hotel hall, the concierge showing no astonishment at her attire. It was his job not to be surprised, just as it is God's to forgive, or Time's to heal.

***

Photographs having been taken a few days earlier, the transaction might have been swift and Henri the proud owner of a Magyar, well, Hungarian passport in the name of Count Heinrich Esterhaffy, born in Budapest in 1951, had there not been a major hiccup: no more titles, at least officially, in Hungary. And nobility was of the essence in this hazy plot.

Sebastian's cousin's resourcefulness allowed the whole procedure to be repeated. So. As in Germany titles are still part of one's family name, Henri now held a passport with the same name but Munich as a birthplace. Naturally, the price had somewhat multiplied, but future benefits were well worth it – or so Sebastian persuaded him.

'A birth certificate will of course be necessary at some

point,' the two rogues pointed out. 'Time for that. I need new stamps and so on.'

Time is what Henri lacked: in one hour, he was expected at the table of Valentine-the-Princess. From Roquebrune to Nice it took approximately that long. But as Count Sàndor had pointed out: to be over-punctual is always a faux pas.

Hence he showered, shaved, changed and called the authentic Count, ashamedly relieved no one answered.

The maître d' swelled out his chest. Overloaded with garlands and cupids, the noble dining room of the Michelin-starred restaurant had been transformed into farcical Disneyland.

Baroness Ella, actually Elena Tresh, born broke before marrying successive millionaires, sailed into the dining room. She waved graciously from one table to the next before removing her elbow-long gloves. With her mane of red hair and sultry figure, dressed Gilda style, she could have been mistaken for Rita Hayworth – from a distance in the dark. As her guests trickled in, she assigned seats from her throne at the head of the table.

To her left, Henri. Next to him, her daughter. To her right, an elderly gentleman whom Henri had caught a glimpse of at the Monte Carlo casino, displaying emerald cuffs. A George Hamilton clone. Despite an all-year-round tan, rather lacklustre. At his side, some top model whose name Henri didn't catch, both 'rent a crowd' specimens. Two more couples were expected to complete the nine-person table, the baroness had forgotten who.

Our hostess swayed two fingers to the staff, indicating they would not wait. This triggered a frantic carousel of waiters slipping small dishes of delicatessen soon removed. The Chantecler was notorious for its nouvelle cuisine.

Not for the first time since his arrival and phony per-sonification, Henri longed to sit at his corner bistro, with a bad steak and a good book. However cuckoo and rather likeable mother and daughter were, you do get tired of theatrics, especially if their gamut of emotion spans A to B.

Valentine's mother embarked on some picturesque tale encapsulating various husbands, many Derbys and travels. From Bratislava to Vienna and from the Carpathians to Rajputana, it was mostly about shooting boars, tigers, chitals…

Henri managed to impress the assembly with his recently acquired knowledge of Hungarian history, dropping names such as the Potocki, the Mittrovsky, the Andrassy and others; that of their castles and stag-hunting records, with just a hint of apology at belonging to the sybarites' louche enclave.

Fireworks would ignite at midnight. It was quarter to. He couldn't stop watching his watch, hoping to be able to slip away in the midst of it.

Ella squeezed his wrist and murmured:

'It's supposedly my daughter's party. Hence I'll spare you my usual digressions about the origins of my title, Counts of the Austrian monarchy in 1682 and then of the Holy Roman Empire in 1701. Please do likewise, would you?'

'No problem!' Henri smiled.

Though her tone bordered on disdain, he liked the lady.

'Dear boy. All of this should not blind you to the fact that my Valentine's a gold-digger. Unless you're a gold mine,' she winked, 'hands off. Might eat you alive.'

Henri remembered Valentine wolfing down the food and crushing lobster shells with her teeth.

'It's hard to know what we inbred aristocrats absorb by

example,' continued Ella. 'It can all become very tenuous.'

Here she addressed him a radiant smile, as if they were exchanging utter trivia, made her bracelets clink, asked for her Danaid glass to be refilled, and proceeded to ignore Henri.

Not so Valentine.

'Mother. Henri's a Count Esterhaffy. Couldn't possibly be a relative of that great flame of yours before you married my father? On a rebound, as they say? Was he not...'

An uproar interrupted this tricky line of questioning. Valentine's ex, nicknamed Prince Hangover, erupted onto the scene.

Clad as a Harlequin, donning an eyepatch, a hunting hat with pheasant feathers and Texan boots, his malicious grin stretched from ear to ear. A bottle of Old Grouse dangling from one hand and a Japanese sword from the other steadied his gait.

'So honoured not to have been invited!' he boomed, throwing several Cartier boxes on the table. 'Marriage annulled, dear ex-wife and mother-in-law. If this isn't cause for celebration, what is? May I introduce my attorney, a most pretty woman?'

Everyone at the table gaped. Except Henri. He knew Karen, having driven her around Paris. Back then, she worked for an escort service in order to finance her law studies. Successfully, it seemed.

Immune to the hostile glances shot at him, plus a connoisseur of human nature, the Prince added:

'You're my guests. Order caviar a gogo, for all I care.'

Valentine, taken by surprise and aback, cupped her face.

Gallantly kissing his former mother-in-law's hand, the Prince hissed:

'Your daughter Valentine is no more Mr van der Bill's daughter than I'm Hannibal's elephant.'

The Prince showed his pretty attorney to a chair and sat opposite her.

'As my client was saying: the marriage is null and void due to a, er, mistaken identity.'

At this point, Henri hooted with laughter. At the same time, he visualised his father's slit throat and his own bleeding wrist, once upon not so long a time.

'Where were we? Oh yes. Celebrating. Maître!' boomed the Prince. 'A magnum of Cristal!'

Sudden dejection seemed to floor him. He looked on the verge of some sort of seizure.

That's how he was and always had been, thought Valentine; episodes of mania followed by depression, the cycle spiralling faster the more he drank. When inebriated, nothing could smother his despondency. He'd feel like watching, but no longer participating, in his own life. The voyeur didn't like what he saw. The coin had flipped. Actually, the Prince started tumbling backwards feeling deflated and defeated – until he drank some more and stopped caring.

It was Ella, of course, who recovered her spirits with swift grace. She retrieved her powder compact. Wrong time to have a shiny nose.

'Dearest, how lovely to see you! Dressed as you are, I'd have recognised you anywhere! Do meet our new friend, Henri, the international gallant Samson Canovas, his model friend, formerly Miss Venezuela, and…'

'Pleasure,' mumbled the Prince, looking most displeased. 'We've met in some brothel or other.'

'How come you didn't barge in here on all fours?' snarled

the Beau, quite livid beneath his orange tan.

A fist fight might have occurred had Sebastian not burst upon the scene, dressed like a Brazilian transvestite, glitter, false eyelashes, the lot.

He patted the Baroness's hand. It had gone limp. Her strength was deserting her. This evening was not going according to plan. She deeply resented departures from scenarios conceived by her. Oh well. This was carnival time after all. With all the composure she could muster, she sing-sang:

'Monsieur. Unless I'm mistaken, you're a chauffeur employed by this distinguished establishment. What gives you the right to ...?'

'The Prince asked me,' he smiled with winning charm (so far as the model was concerned). With a theatrical bow: 'Ladies and gentlemen. I have a not-altogether-honest cousin. Among his illegal but lucrative activities, that of detective. Employed by the Prince. The latter's contention is corroborated. Valentine is not her official father's daughter.'

By now, all heads were turned towards the Baroness's table. Conversations had abated.

'Milady, you married Mr van der Bill quite pregnant by another one of your suitors in order to endow her with an American nationality. Noble intention. Credible, as premature births are nothing out of the ordinary. But then, you made a mistake, as we all do. In this case, the detail that makes the perfect lie so improbable was...'

Ella tried to stand up, swivelled and fainted.

Henri jumped to his feet and knelt at hers. An ambulance was called. The Prince made a swerving exit, followed by Sebastian. The old fox and the young model started kissing.

Guests applauded enthusiastically, believing the whole razzmatazz to have been staged for their entertainment.

The Baroness recovered fast.

Back in her bedroom, she called for Henri and her daughter. In the pose of Dumas's *Dame aux Camélias*, reclining on a divan with a weary mien, she asked them to sit down.

'Children,' she purred, 'what you heard is true. Meaning, dear Henri, that you might well be Valentine's half-brother or something. Yes. I did love that larger-than-life man surrounded by gypsies whom people called Plaffy, compounding "Pauli Filius" – the son of Paul, something biblical, search me. Mesmerising character. He was joyous and generous – though cribbed by debts. A pathological womaniser. It's 1938. No time to marry a Magyar, Esterhaffy or not, let alone to give birth in Budapest.'

Valentine, for a welcome change, shut up.

'It is also true that I belong to a generation and a world where lies were commonplace so long as you didn't let your aplomb shatter. Appearances cemented reality!'

She sighed. Voluptuously, Henri thought.

'Do our own lies enlighten us about those others? Back then they did. Disorder becomes taboo in tumultuous times. Games were our shelter – within the bounds of convention. An elastic concept. Faith, in those days, was a thing with feathers...'

Valentine looked as if standing on stilts. When she finally talked, she did so like a sleepwalker. But in spite of her vapid expression, she again flabbergasted Henri.

'Mother is right. Our lives were a succession of small secrets. Money helped, as usual. But then: one does get tired of roaming from cruises to continents, from casinos to social circuses, from gondolas to golf courses. Mother and I confused filling voids with fulfilment.'

A knock at the door. Valentine leaped up to open it. Sebastian, now in jeans and a white shirt. It was almost one o'clock in the morning.

He respectfully asked if anyone needed his services. Casually, he apologised for the 'incident' earlier on. His carrying an ice bucket in which swam a bottle of Black Label mollified the Baroness.

Having seen enough of Sebastian, of heart-shaped balloons, and of the hotel, Henri sneaked out and hailed a taxi.

'To Cannes please. The Carlton.'

Valentine's Day coinciding with Mardi Gras in 1980, people would be tipsy, which would benefit his newly acquired swindling skills. If the wheels of justice didn't spin, the wheels of fortune might. With a new identity, time for action. And at long last, some sex. He'd forgotten all about it.

'At the roulette table, two Spaniards sail towards me,' he'd tell Seb the next day. 'They had seen me "at work" in Monte Carlo. I of course assure them I'm a penniless employee asked to play the buffoon for a Hungarian Count in order to trace his long-lost daughter, hence to infiltrate the "milieu". Nothing like the truth to create disbelief. They propose a deal. Should I initiate them to my *martingale*, they'd finance the whole operation. Oh? Gains will be divided in half, but not losses. That didn't sound too credible. But the guys had more experience than me – unless miracles are a factor of randomness. In short: 400,000 francs was equitably shared.'

Impressed, Seb ordered a round of pastis.

'Another couple joined our little group. At four in the morning, I realised that winning or losing is ultimately monotonous. No mesmerising doll in sight, presumably otherwise engaged at such late hour, I scampered.'

This time, no escape from fraternal shoulder-slapping.

***

Back in the Negresco, Henri showered and packed. Manipulation compounded delusion. This was getting spooky. He called the early-rising Count Sàndor.

As convincingly as he could, he summed up latest events. The quintessence: Baroness Tresch had admitted that Valentine was indeed his child. Mission accomplished.

'Have you fallen in love with her?' coughed the old man.

In prey to disjointed emotions, Henri's heart went blank. Daughter? Mother?

He needed no mirror to appraise himself from afar, lying on a king-size bed, in a bathrobe with a crown embroidered on its upper pocket, looking healthy and wealthy. A clown brimming over with complacency.

At the other end, the Count hadn't lost his train of thought.

'Right, my friend. Here are my instructions. Do whatever may be necessary to lure my daughter to Paris. Use whatever bait you must. I want to see her before I die. Rather soon, the medics tell me. But at least I'll pass away with twenty kilos lost,' he chuckled. 'Meanwhile, stay where you are. Understood?'

How was Henri to tell him he had usurped the Count's family name or about his fraudulent activities? How was he to confess that he had no desire whatsoever to return to his former identity or to resume his mousy existence? Furthermore, how to explain he had tasted the juicy fruit of illegality and savoured it?

He could.

He'd fly back to Paris and explain all. Wittily told, the story would titillate the old man. All in all, no harm had been done, right? Also, the crooked hoaxes had allowed Henri to keep expenses reasonable. Agreed, the Negresco suite bill was another ball game ... but an intrinsic part of the deal, frankly!

Was he still able to fake frankness?

Fabrication feeding on habit, habits a disease, the faculty to lie spreads like a tumour. Like most vices, it's a mechanism. You must keep the car in top gear lest you crash. Meanwhile, your compass goes wild.

Hunger chased such musings away. Where to hide?

The probabilities of Valentine and her mother appearing at the Opera restaurant were slim, considering the owner's hostile attitude towards a rich tramp. Henri sauntered in its direction, mirthlessly.

On the morrow of February 14th, after all the festivities, the place was fortunately not only open, but empty.

He had taken Baedeker's 1902 red guide to the Riviera with him. Peace at last.

Having ordered his best meal for a while – normal food – he reclined and smoked, ineffably happy to be alone.

The charming owner offered up some of their house brandy after his coffee. Henri thanked her with effusion.

'Do you mind if my husband Maurice joins you? I must do an inventory. He can't help. Arthritis, you know?'

'Gladly, Mrs...'

'Ariane.'

A short while later, a stiff but handsome man, nearing his eighties, shuffled to Henri's table.

His eyes scintillated with intelligence. His face, with candour.

'An honour,' said Henri, rising to shake hands.

Mr Maurice wasn't voluble. What a relief after excessive hen-quacking. But the silence didn't last for long as, noticing Henri's Baedeker, he exclaimed:

'What a surprise to see a young man carrying what used to be one of my bibles! Is your name Count Ester… something?'

'Forget it. Henri.'

'Henri. I'm an atheist, thus you must, I pray (smile) forgive my reference to a sacred book. Thing is that I'm an actor – well, was.'

'Do tell,' he responded, hoping for a monosyllabic answer. No such luck.

'I'll skip my beginnings, as arduous then as now for actors. Years later, I wrote a play in which I played the leading part. A flop. It was the owner of an obscure cultural magazine with a dwindling readership, need I add, who came to my rescue.'

Mr Maurice's fingers joined in a pyramid, his hands dreamy.

'Won't the ramblings of a has-been bore you?'

'No,' retorted the by now Pavlovian liar.

'All right then. Mr McNamar's boundless vitality fitted an ogre-like personality. Inhabited by a passion for the arts and an invincible faith in undiscovered gifts, he financed my next play and performance.'

Henri yawned, the accumulated tension abating.

'You are too lank and if I may venture, exhausted. Are

you in trouble?'

'Yes.'

'Bad?'

'Don't know.'

The old actor's voice was soothing. His manners, delicate.

Upon waking up, his head on his arms, both Ariane and Maurice were engaged in conversation and laughing.

Henri observed them from under half-closed lashes. These two gave another meaning to marriage or, say, companionship.

'Invigorating snacks is what we need!'

Maurice tilted his head.

'Snacks! She's bound to bring back a gourmet plate of baked clams, snails with garlic, what have you…'

'Apologies. How uncouth of me to doze off…'

'Feel at home. A childless home…'

Why hadn't he been blessed with such parents? That said, there was something strange about the couple. They treated each other with utmost caution – or was it precaution – as if the slightest departure from restraint might cause something to crack.

'Please resume where you left it,' Henri did not exactly plead.

'Oh well. My second play was a kind of persiflage about Dante's *Inferno*. McNamar being a control freak, we fell out over trivialities. End of a relationship. Sad.'

Ariane came back with a tray of irresistible tit-bits.

'So glad you get along,' she hushed.

'Thereafter … to produce and promote without money is tough. Not one to take what he considered lack of loyalty gracefully, McNamar attacked me in the press and in private with ferocious vindictiveness.'

'Sorry...'

'Don't be. One must always be grateful for having been granted first opportunities. Besides, as my wife says, the past has no future, so why dwell upon it?'

'... and the present is a mirage,' added Ariane. 'Can't wait for it to be over!'

Maurice smiled dismissively.

'We bought this restaurant because of the proximity of Place Garibaldi's to the theatre. Here I was able to adapt *Le Roman d'un Tricheur*, playing the role of The Cheat as the author Sacha Guitry had done in the cinematographic version in 1936.'

Henri stood up.

'Mind if I accompany you to your hotel? Need the exercise.'

'*Volontiers.*'

The walk back was pleasurable. The lanterns on the Promenade des Anglais cast a jaundiced glow. The moon, blurred by mist, coated the sea with pearly ripples. Their steps failed to resonate on the pavement. Utter silence until the church bells began to chime seven o'clock.

Maurice seemed impervious to his surroundings. The disinterest was reciprocal; no one paused to notice someone as anodyne as a middle-sized elderly man wearing an unremarkable coat, a crumpled hat, and no glasses. The song 'I'm a Melancholy Man' by The Moody Blues bubbled up in Henri's head.

'McNamar's vendetta had made me doubt my every step. In order to reassure myself, I became a compulsive liar to test improbable audiences. I invented a new autobiography; fabricated dramas in order to elicit interest; confessed imaginary deeds; disguised myself with alter egos ... as did you the other day, I was told. Amusing.'

Out of breath, he stalled.

'Talking about my wife: she nearly left me. I bent silly details of everyday life in the urge to distort it. The day she examined banknotes suspecting them to be counterfeit, the line had obviously been crossed.'

Here he laughed bittersweetly.

'Did you find it easy to stop?' Henri inquired.

'No. You get hooked on risky games. Not that they're difficult, most of the time. People are so very gullible. Then there's a phenomenon called self-reinforcement or some such, whereby whatever you do confirms your pretence. It can be cruel. An example? You pretend to be gravely ill. Then you meet someone to whom you've told this, but you're actually looking in the pink. Thinking you're being stoical, he or she redoubles the compassion.'

Called belief perseverance, thought Henri.

'A footnote. Lies weren't what kept me alive. They were what kept me alone. So much so that I tried to kill myself.'

Whereupon he turned on his heel.

***

In the Negresco's hall, a most unwanted welcome committee. The Baroness, Valentine and Sebastian were sipping pink champagne. Their mood suggested it wasn't their first bottle.

'Hulloooo everybody,' grumbled Henri. 'Do forgive me but I need to freshen up. And then, an early night…'

'Without you I'm going nowhere,' purred Valentine, pouting expertly.

'You are our only true friend here!' exclaimed Ella. 'Don't spoil our fun!'

'My cousin has something for you,' added Sebastian with a mischievous glance. 'And me, an idea to go with it!' Addressing the ladies, he winked.

'Young Count's turning into a gourmet.'

The mere idea of more food made Henri feel sick. Then again – wasn't he on a mission? Having lied to the Count by omission, he could not face desertion.

***

In the car, Valentine and Ella sung along to the music, full volume non-stop. A cacophonic nightmare.

Seb's cousin had dressed up. A tweed suit and bow tie! Only the golf club was missing.

A pseudo-butler produced canapés and martinis on silver-plated trays.

Did the cousin, other than a knack for entertainment, have a name? Henri suddenly wondered.

'I'm a source of useless information, miladys,' he started perorating. 'Did you know, for instance, that when they shot *The Graduate*, Anne Bancroft was only six years older than Dustin Hoffman? Hmm? Did you know that Lincoln had a secretary called Kennedy and that JFK's secretary was named Lincoln? And that both presidents were succeeded by a Johnson?'

Helping himself to a very large glass of Burgundy, basking in the attention, he pursued:

'Did you know that Buzz Aldrin's mother's maiden name was Moon? That "a blue moon" is a second full moon in the same month? That the koala bear isn't actually a bear, but a marsupial? That all polar bears are left-handed?'

Faced with blank expressions, he sighed.

'Right. I believe you're more interested in titles. Did you know that the Duke of Devonshire, whose stately home Chatsworth is actually in Derbyshire, owes his title to a spelling mistake? *Bon d'accord.*'

Sebastian whispered that the man had more in store. Henri, at this point, would have given any kingdom for a bed.

'Here's some good news. Do you know that women use twenty thousand words a day to men's seven thousand?'

Valentine interrupted:

'Might be because, whilst men want to understand the world, we wish to understand people? I read somewhere that eighty percent of autistic people are men as they tend to store facts in a maniac way.'

Also known as Asperger's syndrome, the cousin reflected. Not such a vanilla bimbo after all. On the other hand, her brain could hardly be compared to a Rubik's Cube, which has more combinations than the miles travelled by light in a century.

Talking of time. This one called for music.

'Do you know,' he said, uncorking a new bottle, 'that in 1977, when Elvis Presley died, there were 170 Elvis impersonators around? By the millennium they amounted to 85,000. Mathematically, this would mean that by 2019 one third of the world's population will be Elvis impersonators.'

The Baroness hiccupped.

'Did you know,' giggled Valentine, 'that a zebra's stripes are white on a black background, as opposed to black on…'

Sebastian pulled Henri's sleeve.

'Enough. Let them talk themselves into a stupor. Off to business.'

***

He leads me into what he euphemistically called the atelier, Henri would recount. On the table, a bunch of green cheques. The first error that strikes me: though in pounds sterling, the heading reads Traveler Cheques. Wrong spelling, you fool, I snap. Besides, cheques issued by such entities are too easily proven false with only the briefest of delays, as they immediately get discounted. Oh, I know what you're up to, Seb. You want me to buy valuables, resell them, and share the proceeds. But you see, if we want to get away with it, get your cousin to reprint all this and invent some obscure bank based in the Caymans or somewhere offshore.

Sebastian looked like someone outwitted at his own game. Since when are you such an expert? he barked. Since I met you, and started thinking along your lines, that's when. I was furious, but just a little. The scheme was simple, after all. Tax authorities rob the taxpayer. Why not swing back? This said, to be a swindler requires permanent attention. Permanent concentration. In other words, permanent stress. Was it worth it?

Were, as Maurice had said, lies an addiction? Having recovered his bearings, Sebastian riposted that 'these kind of cheques usually don't get presented to banks. Mostly, they get exchanged between traders. Another form of traffic, my friend…'

And so on. Sebastian laughed. 'Let's take the ladies to the Moulin de Mougins for the most expensive dinner ever. Don't forget your English accent! I'll be the host,' he grinned, grabbing £100 cheques. 'It's Friday – the best day of the week, as banks are closed for forty hours, remember?'

Later, much later that evening, the cousin – called Cyril, by the way – having volunteered to drive the ladies back, Seb and I play at Monte Carlo. We have cashed the fake cheques against plastic chips. I ostentatiously play large sums staking on all numbers at once. Whilst ostentatiously lamenting my losses, Seb amasses the gains on the winning number. Gains thus annul losses, our objective. After a few hours, he cashes in the sums I have illegally exchanged against the travellers cheques. We leave separately. Fortunately, our ploy has gone unnoticed compared to what Arabs have been gambling all the while.

The day after was worse than a hangover. That recurrent dream of stepping off a cliff had turned obsessive. On top of it, and of me, a dishevelled, naked Valentine. *Bon*: she had been spread-eagled on my bed, fishnets, garters and all, her silky skin oozing with an intoxicating perfume. She's been a tigress and oh, was I hungering for sex. So I went wild too. Who was the predator, who the consenting victim, can't remember. Rape or rapture? Ditto. One thing I knew: woman can moan and squeal on command, but when their every muscle quivers in epileptic spasms, it's for real. I further discovered what it is like to feel and look like shit – I had become one. Breakfast never made it into my stomach.

An hour or so later, marinating in a Jacuzzi, his remorse diluted by two Bloody Marys, Henri chuckled: the absurd thought that he had now added pseudo-incest to injury was both hilarious and horrific. If such extraordinary things could happen to such an ordinary man, where did the limit lie?

Besides. Wasn't life in a five-star hotel meant to be an abdication of responsibilities – like a cruise ship, or indeed jail? What date was it? February sixteenth? Seventeenth? He remembered an interview with some astronaut. He'd admitted that the most difficult thing back on Earth, after weeks of zero gravity in a controlled environment, was readapting to choices: what to do or not to do.

Oh well. Time to buy a present for Valentine. Another for Maurice and Ariane. Why not for the naïve baroness too? A safe full of illicit money, obtained by stealth – not violence – would allow for atonement.

The problem: how to sneak out without being harpooned by the bewitching witches? He had taken the precaution of bringing a change of clothes (the trouser pocket stuffed with cash) to the spa, but... Of course! In the masseur's cabin, a white coat was bound to hang, and then: what were staff entrances for, if not to exit discreetly?

Fresh air! First stop, the Lamartine bookshop. He knew what he'd buy Maurice and his wife: *L'Homme au Désir d'Amour Lointain*, the best novel ever. Then, *Le Roman d'un Tricheur* (one for himself, another for Sebastian). It being an old-fashioned bookshop that didn't just store novelties (and those for only three weeks), he found the lot.

For Valentine and Ella? Hermès was a safe bet ... even though they didn't sell dominatrix lingerie, ha ha. There he spotted a superb travelling bag in the thinnest, softest calf leather. He had it embossed with the initials S.E. topped with the Esterhaffy's coat of arms.

Ambling lazily towards the marketplace, rejoicing in a beer and a newspaper in some simple café, he was startled by an abrupt screeching of wheels, followed by screams.

The very taxi driver who had picked him up from the

airport milled his arms like a clock gone mad. He had run over a dog. Though awful, the hysteria on the street bore something comical.

In a flash, Henri recalled the maître d' at the Chantecler telling him that Valentine, a year earlier, had giggled watching a similar scene from the restaurant's window. The taxi driver recognised Henri and gestured to him for help. Henri, in another flash, remembered the commotion, back in Paris, when he had hit the bicycle. He rushed over.

A crimson-faced policeman looked rabid.

'Wait a moment!' commanded Henri. 'Calm down. This guy doesn't kill dogs on purpose!'

'How would you know?' snapped the cop, eyeing the orange Hermès shopping bags with a snide glance.

An old lady was crunched on the sidewalk, wailing.

She admitted that she'd forgotten the leash and that her dog was temperamental.

Things settled down. Like an automaton, Henri agreed to step into the taxi.

'Thanks man. Shall we drive to where the most scented mimosas grow?' he smiled. 'Take a walk...?'

Henri had forgotten all about mimosas. The fickle realisation that he had spent most of his stay in Nice in cars or on chairs crossed, then departed, his mind.

'...but first we need a stiff one! My name's Robert.'

Booze. Of course. Part and parcel of sedentary debauch.

Half an hour later, they stopped in a rustic place overlooking the bay. All the way, Robert, a compulsive talker, had talked. Lost in an emotional haze, Henri hadn't paid much attention.

'You know, *mon vieux*, it's so rare to meet a good listener! My accordion-playing career or my trekking makes people doze off, would you believe it?'

Nothing like misunderstandings to forge a bond.

During their long walk, the ex-taxi-driver told the not-yet-ex-taxi-driver the whole story, from d'Ormessson to Count Sàndor, from Sebastian to Valentine, not forgetting Cyril and the Baroness. The very notion of reality, obfuscated by lies, seemed to recover substance by being put into words. The urge had been irresistible.

Robert never interrupted. After a long silence, he said:

'Your story reminds me of a play I saw many years ago in our small old-town theatre. *Roman d'un Tricheur*. At first, very entertaining. Then, its more profound meaning hits you.'

Amazing. The mention of that book seemed inescapable.

'What's honesty, in the end? If you get away with lies, why stop? We're not talking about murder, right?'

Robert choked. He must have remembered the dog and the distraught old woman.

'Thing is that when things are too easy, you stop taking precautions. Bending the law makes you think you're above them. Ah, forget it. Let's drive back. With "Stabat Mater" by Vivaldi, if you don't mind.'

In Nice, Robert turned around:

'Your secret's safe with me. But a word of advice: Cyril is a manipulating scoundrel. He pulls all the strings, including rather stupid Sebastian's. I don't trust the guy. Never did. Nothing's good enough for him. Never will.'

Henri decided to walk back to the Negresco on the beach, barefoot. The mistral wind lashed his face. Time to leave. Fast. But first: how to convince Valentine to come to Paris with him? She had, at some point, squeaked that she hated the place. Painful memories; which, she did not say.

Did their torrid night afford him some leverage? Failing that, the lavish present bought at Hermès? Would her mother object, or else, be cajoled into lending her support (another lavish present)? Even come along – why not? The Count would have both for the price of one...

His cynical musing was interrupted by the sight of Sebastian and Valentine kissing near the shore. Were they laughing at the same time? Looked like it.

***

Henri hastened back to the hotel, his heart running amok. What the hell was going on?

Back in his rooms, he switched on the finally re-connected television for background noise.

Thundering knocks on the door. Ubiquitous Sebastian.

'Henri. We must leave for Roquebrune at once! My cousin has a plan. Most ingenuous. Quite a heist, in fact.'

'Don't waste your breath. Or else suffuse your girlfriend with it. Valentine, is it not? I'm out of here.'

Seb flinched.

'Dear no-Count-at-all, you are indispensable. And may I add, in no position to let us down.'

Henri started scribbling frenetically.

Threatening or not, his words triggered off a resolution. I wanted to know who the mastermind in that crazy story was. A set-up from the beginning? Had Valentine and Seb been under the same blanket, in every sense, all along? In league with the obnoxious cousin? Anyway: I too changed tone. Sounds too intriguing not to intrigue me, I smiled. Seb, reassured, winked. I suspected Robert the taxi driver to be right: he was no genius.

Upon arriving at the cousin's, the latter rushes out to welcome us. The answer to my question, if not on the wall, might have been on his T-shirt:

I'M NOT BOSSY. I AM THE BOSS.

His manner was too mellifluous for comfort. What was these people's ulterior motive? And did the cousins not look and act like twins, come to think of it?

Henri was soon enlightened: they wanted him to steal Valentine's jewellery – before her ex could reclaim it, on the grounds of an annulled marriage.

'We understand you stooped so low as to have, er, an intimate relationship with Her Highness... It should simplify matters. All we need is the room key. Safe-cracking is one of our expertises,' hissed Cyril...

'... as are outlets for stolen goods or offshore accounts,' Seb added.

Really! Making them an organised gang, or part thereof, and him, a pawn and a fool? They had more than enough to blackmail him. Probably all on tape, on camera – probably both.

Now familiar with gambling, Henri refused point-blank. Bluff. Whereupon the two rogues waved their trump card:

'Count Sàndor Esterhaffy won't be too happy to be deprived of the pleasure of his daughter's company shortly before his last puff,' sighed Cyril with theatrical regret.

Sebastian chewed his fingernails.

So they knew! Confirming Henri's previous suspicion.

Valentine. An innocent lamb indeed. She probably was part of the 'scheme': it would allow her to recover quite a fortune from the insurance. And everyone would always believe that a Princess came adorned with authentic stones, be they false. A win-win situation!

A trapped animal's response is aggression, is it not? He opted for the human version: cunning.

'Understood. Will do as you ask. But after that, please, let me return to my former life. I miss it!'

The truth was no longer an issue. Or rather, an increasingly abstract one.

The lookalikes looked at each other. Henri's forlorn expression fooled them.

'Deal.'

Henri pretended he needed fresh air and jumped into Seb's car. He always left the keys inside it, he had noticed.

He drove back at a leisurely pace. Numbed, yes, engulfed in vicarious shame, also, but feeling idiotically happy.

***

In front of the Negresco, flashing police cars. The so-called cousins had wasted no time. Pure routine. Really? They let him go. Weird but on reflection, logical. The whole thing was meant as a warning.

In the hall, the Baroness turned a cold shoulder.

Next to her, Valentine acted all velvety.

Behind them, the concierge with a stern mien.

Something was very wrong.

Henri headed to the bar, hoping for the indifference various martinis usually bestow. They were of course followed by the backlash: intense anguish. He was trapped in a trap of his own making – one he had willingly fallen into. Fatalism, no longer an option.

What was? A conversation with Mr Maurice. The only sane person around.

Head high, spirit low, he enters the Opera restaurant.

It's six or seven o'clock. Just before opening hour. Melancholy Maurice sits alone. His face lights up.

'Bonsoir! Pleasure to see you!'

Henri lets himself fall on a chair.

'A drink?'

'No. Really not. Never drank so much in my life as in Nice!' Henri smiles. 'Or perhaps only one glass of…'

'Bottle on the table. Now tell me why you came.'

Henri, discomfited, inhales deeply.

'Wherever I go, people you'd rather not meet tell me about *Le Roman d'un Tricheur*, praising your performance, by the way. I bought the book but haven't found time to read it.'

Maurice shrugged.

'Oh! Story's really quite simple. A boy steals money from his family's grocery shop to buy marbles in order to play with his friends. He's caught and punished: no dinner for him that night. We're talking about poor people to whom a meal is a special event. The boy is sent to bed. He can hear his siblings and parents relishing mushrooms – with sauce. A feast! Well. They all die: the mushrooms were venomous.'

Henri imagines the lack of morality to the tale in a flash.

'The boy's conclusion: it pays off to steal. It saved his life. His name in the novel is "The Cheat". His mother's unscrupulous cousin takes charge of him but only to snap up his meagre inheritance.'

Henri cups his face with his hands. The orphan being placed in the custody of a dragon relative makes him shiver. Compassion floods Maurice's eyes.

'Shall I go on?'

'…'

'So. The grown-up boy takes on all sorts of jobs. In

Monte Carlo he meets an old Countess with whom he has a fling – he's now a gigolo. No scruples…'

Jesus, thinks Henri. Have I become an archetype?

'I skip the episode in the army. Still in Monaco, he becomes a croupier, meets a professional swindler who, after a passionate night spent together, convinces him to take part in a jewellery robbery.'

How perversely could fiction overlap with reality?

'*Bon*. This one persuades him to fix the cards at some table or another. He does. She wins constantly and they agree to a marriage of convenience … among thieves. When he's no longer willing to play along, she loses all her money. Then, it gets nasty.'

Observing Henri, he again asked if he should go on. Same acquiescent silence. This time, emphatic.

'Nasty and sad. Because, when he was wounded in the First Word War, a man rescued him. The same guy turns up at the casino one night. Not recognising his saviour, The Cheat turns him into another victim of the usual tricks. Upon realising his mistake, ashamed to his heart's core, The Cheat reverts to an honest job. That of a security officer. Would you believe it?'

'No,' riposted Henri.

Mr Maurice nodded.

'Nor did I. In my version, the man commits suicide. Self-disgust pushes him over the razor's edge.'

'How?' Henri asked, his voice betraying morbid curiosity.

'There are many ways. I researched.'

Clients trickled in. Ariane left them alone. Henri watched her closely. He admired her and envied Maurice.

'Let's sit in a corner,' murmured the latter. 'You need help.'

'What kind?'

'You are depressed, my friend. Call it despondent. The definition of both, in my humble opinion, is...'

'Self-pessimism,' retorted Henri, quoting d'Ormesson.

'Well put. Snap out of it. You are good-looking, clever and resourceful. Leave this town. No good. And perhaps, do as the protagonist of the *Roman d'un Tricheur* did: The Cheat, aged fifty-four, writes his memoirs in a café. Writing is a catharsis. This is what I told my disciples – yes I had quite a few, once upon a time. Many heeded my advice.'

(Henri didn't need to. He had tossed down his mingled thoughts and mixed feelings shortly after arriving in Nice. Which is why, in this story, there are various intervals recounted by him. Even the most foxy liar needs some sort of release from guilt. Writing, as all diarists know, is more discreet than a confessional. Only a sheet of paper to unburden to.)

He left. It was getting loud in that restaurant, and he couldn't stand noise anymore. Nor the thought of solitude.

On the street, he spotted a telephone booth. Rummaging in his pockets he found Robert the taxi driver's number.

'I was expecting your call. Come over. A *bouillabaisse* on the stove!'

It was nearby. Henri craved the sensation that comes only when you're surrounded by a normal family, whatever that might be, sitting in a cosy kitchen.

None of this materialised.

Robert, his big belly covered by an apron, opened the door and led him to a freezing dining room.

'Sorry for the mess. That's how it looks like when your wife has died and your son has run away.'

He beamed. What was there to beam about?

'So sorry. Should I not have…?'

'As I said, I was expecting you. My son – as I told you when we first met – is an adolescent. He'll be back when hungry. I'm not worried.'

The man's insouciance and warm welcome lifted Henri's spirits. The *bouillabaisse* was fantastic. For some reason, the conversation drifted to Mr Maurice. Henri expressed his fondness and awe of him. Robert's reaction took him aback.

'Do you know, Henri, how often that man attempted suicide?'

'What?'

'At least four times. Careful, Henri. The man is toxic.'

'Impossible!' exclaimed Henri.

Robert looked away.

'You're a newcomer here. Shall I show you an interview Maurice gave to the press? You know what we all thought? That he's desperate for attention. Here's the article. I dug it out today. Do as you wish. I need some time prepare a prune soufflé,' he smiled.

The interview? Maurice, talking about his plays, insists their endings to be the same: 'voluntary death'. The only dignified one. 'God hasn't created mankind; men have created God. Many gods, in fact, in a vain attempt to accept the finality of life and its injustice. Therefore, we have a divine right to determine the end of his passage between two voids.'

The woman journalist has naturally fallen under his charm.

'I understand you made an attempt yourself. Why would such a handsome man, with such a colourful past, and a wonderful wife, wish to die?'

'Death wishes are common among lucid romantics.'

'What about the devastating effect your passing away is bound to have on those close to you?'

'Close?'

'Yes. Close.'

'The closest ones in life remain strangers. Watch someone sleeping next to you. Do you know anything, anything at all about the intimate world that person is immersed in, a world utterly hermetic to you, sharing the same pillow?'

'What a dismal view of things!'

'But not veiled. Lady, life is a tragicomedy. *Cette triste gaîté dont on rit quand on ne peut plus en pleurer.* When you've had enough, it's time to go. Want some advice?'

Henri visualised the journalist's dilemma. This was macabre but ... she was young. The outrageous sells. Mr Maurice had never granted an interview. She had to seize her opportunity.

'All right. Your thoughts on suicide, Monsieur.'

'Not thoughts. Facts. Most attempts fail. I should know. Deliberately or not is a debate beyond my competence. People who cut their wrists often suspect they'll be found before it's too late. People who pretend to hang themselves don't know how to tie a noose properly. People who overdose on pills, generally combined with alcohol, end up throwing up. Besides, it was easier in the Marilyn Monroe days with drugs like Nembutal and the like on the market. You need to be a vet to get hold of efficient stuff. As to the old hosepipe attached to the exhaust? Carbon monoxide has been filtered out. Similarly, the head-in-the-oven routine makes no sense with natural gas. Of course, there are opioids like Fentanyl. But who is trained to self-inject it? The hairdryer in the bathtub? Again: the ground fault interruption system, or GFIC, has made this method obsolete. Then there is jumping off a bridge or a rooftop – better backwards – or shooting yourself. All of it a mess. Most candidates for suicide are cowards. Mainly the ones who act with so-called premeditation. A real suicide is spontaneous. I should know!'

Maurice went on to enumerate famous people who had committed suicide. Hemingway, Stefan Zweig, Rothko, Virginia Woolf, Van Gogh, Jean Seberg and her father-figure husband, Romain Gary. The latter an interesting case of identity theft, by the way, as he stole his own by adopting a pseudonym and leading a triple life. Too complicated. Had all of them become victims of emotionally lethal expectations, Henri shivered? Just like his father's words, 'I'm proud of you already', had loaded him with ballast?

Cheerful Robert brandished his dessert. What was the matter with him? Had he learnt or been born to be happy?

They chit-chatted about this and that, had a laugh or two. Violin concertos notwithstanding, Henri felt anguished when he got back to the Negresco. He'd phone Count Sàndor. There was still time to prevent the fissure from expanding into a chasm. Still a decent time to call, given the old man's insomnia.

But what he saw made him recoil. Two policemen were engaged in heated conversation with the director. Seated in nearby armchairs, three sun-glassed men in black. Cyril's squires? He stepped back and used the now familiar back entrance.

Upon reaching his suite, shit: no key.

The door was half-open. Shit again.

The worst was yet to come in the shape and form of a

wheelchair facing the window.

'Switch on the lights.'

If the voice was chagrined, the eyes threw metallic sparks. As to his aspect: spectral. Ashen skin, bony frame, salient cheeks. The shadow of his former self, but not of his soul.

'Sit down.'

'I can explain,' started Henri. 'In truth, I was about to call you to explain it all...'

'Truth? Don't you dare mention that word again!' the Count now hollered. 'Had a long talk with Valentine. Dispatched her to Paris. Do tamp and light my cigar. Fingers atrophied.'

Henri did as told. The Count massaged his left arm with a grimace.

'I have lived through many wars. Traitors galore. But you! You, in whom I put faith, duping me! It's repugnant. Repugnant! No amount of excuses can exonerate such perverted hubris! Imagine this. In my last will you would have been my heir, along with that mercenary blonde. But then you usurp my family name, a name that stands for pride and honour.'

He coughed and spat.

'Remove your things, especially the dirty money in your safe. Wouldn't wish to be soiled by any of it. I'm at a loss for words.'

So was Henri. Humiliation and guilt galvanised him. His stomach dyspeptic, his brain throbbing, he faced doom.

'Shame on you, Henri. Shame on you.'

Whereupon the Count sunk into what seemed slumber.

Henri took nothing at all. He ran to the lift remembering, for some absurd reason, Cyril telling him that the lift company Otis transported, in one week only, the equivalent of the planet's population in its cabins worldwide.

Same procedure: the staff exit.

Sebastian's car keys in the ignition.

He raced off towards the mountains, the words 'I'm proud of you already' looping through his every fibre; accelerated some more, then crashed against a tree, head- and heart-on.

If declared an accident, his last lie.

A stunt?

No. A mediocre end.

2

D's DOG

I

It wasn't difficult.

When not exaggeratedly nuanced or subtle, we do understand human language. With my Master, no problem. His barking a lot helped.

We associate sounds with gestures to fathom meaning. Even in this respect, deciphering it didn't require the mind of some Champollion. D's scope of body language matched his vocabulary: a restricted gamut. Good vs. Bad. Tremendous vs. Crooked. Smart vs. Sleazy. The gestures were also unequivocal: the accusing index finger vs. the thumbs-up. Both linked to make a looped point. Arms outstretched to embrace no one but himself.

He rambled on, yes, repeated the same lines, yes again, but even harangues were bearable thanks to his raucous voice. Some denounced his shallow rhetoric and called his style dyslexic... My opinion? The simpler, the better.

He adored me with endearing incompetence. To think he was accused of despising women! Let me sneeze coquettishly. My name is Pandora. I'm a Labrador. Never ever dreamt of being treated so well. One might hastily conclude it's because I never contradicted my Master. Hastily.

Brought up in a semi-military school, D was conditioned to expect and show discipline. Loyalty being the essence, he would take any swerving therefrom as a personal affront. And what are we, the Best of Dogs, all about? Exactly. Why do the police, for instance, choose us? Can you imagine a King Charles or a poodle sniffing out drugs, pointing at bombs? Please.

Where was I? Yes – my Master's reliance upon me.

I'd been bought by D's French cook as a puppy. When NATO food became politically incorrect, she was fired. A fat indemnity stipulated Yvette had to leave me behind.

Having replaced her with a Russian lady of kosher inclinations (the new gastronomic rage) D became aware of my canine cleverness (correlation always hits you provided you look long enough).

His children had invented neither dynamite nor the wheel, forgive me for sneezing so. I, on the other hand, displayed qualities associated with the over-gifted: to learn skills fast; to pick up and interpret non-verbal cues swifter still; to draw inferences that others need to have mapped out; never to let trivialities like sex impede concentration. Plus, relentless alertness being quintessential, needing little sleep. Not least, D suffering from mysophobia – the endless handshaking he was subjected to entailed frantic antibacterial gel consumption – he was also pleased that no squeezing of my nifty paw was needed to seal a deal. (His tweeting that "the good thing about the Ebola epidemic is NO MORE SHAKING HANDS" had caused acrimonious consternation...)

Neither his kids nor his employees were allowed to touch me. D was the boss. Everybody's boss.

Did he realise I wasn't so colour blind as not to notice his similarity to Tintin?

Bottom line for the time being: after years of working around the clock, neglecting his family, his diet, even pillow talk, he had become the chairman of a company called THE WORLD. No less.

Suddenly – not gradually – he had enough.

Not that he was lonely at the top, as the cliché goes. He felt lonely *tout court*. Fed up. The problem: D could buy everything, activate remote controls to make the unthinkable happen – but respect was dwindling fast.

Hounded by the press, bodyguards, ex-wives, no respite, no peace. Except with me, that is.

Power wore him out. He lost weight. He also lost some hair (not really a problem since he donned a toupee). Most significantly: he became bored.

THE WORLD disenchanted him. The powers-that-had-always-been thwarting his ambition to change it, he suspected that pragmatism would be defeated. (His recurrent refrain, 'I'm no idealist. I'm a realist,' suddenly sounded as dated as a Tino Rossi song.)

Not only had he intended, furiously, to cross lines. He had intended to shift them. Yet: were there any lines left? 'I'm in it to win it,' another slogan, was fading into insignificance. He no longer knew whether he was revered for himself rather than for what he represented. What's more:

he started caring.

When disillusioned, you are destitute.

So you live in immense villas, fly around in private jets, own golf clubs, private islands or satellites. But at night, what?

Outside your room, security rogues; opposite your windows, cameras, journalists, TV reporters, and above the whole commotion, helicopters. The noise! Security isn't in numbers. Death threats pour through your letterbox or the internet. Tiresome.

Fortunately, he couldn't stand the Russian/Kosher food anymore either. He had publicised eating it day in, night out to please his shareholders.

Woof. Was I glad! But even reverting to Max D's hamburgers (a chain he of course owned) didn't lift up his spirits.

Flanking his public appearances, I had become acutely aware of his despondency. Putting my muzzle on his knee no longer elicited a smile. My Master was at loss.

II

One strange day, D started to take me to strange places. Hospitals. Care homes. Foundations.

At first, good fun: what a graphic, tail-spiking change from my charmed life. What a culture shock, if I may use so two-legged an expression! The companions I met had never travelled, never been fed steak tartare or shampooed with lavender soap. They were streetwise; I, a thousand-acre spoilt diva. Needless to say – as some say before embarking on a long discourse – their icy shoulder bruised me. D sensed it. Beneath his brash and blunt personae, he was, at heart, intuitive. Our Achilles' heel: need for recognition.

'Don't you give a damn. We're the best! Believe me!'

He repeated this thrice, as was his wont whenever making a statement.

Fine with me: as poorly articulate as my Master, I fear confusion. Or is it hubris? Intelligent I am, yes, but no intellectual. D respected this. Yet I must admit to have begun purring like a...no! No! His tone changed to one of command:

'Pandora. Keep vigilant. Smart. I realise you see far better and further than your kin. Can't fool me, lady.'

Thank Wolf for Sam Carton.

***

Whereas D was about 490 dog-years old, Sam and I were about the same age (seven times five, in human years). More importantly: we understood each other.

Carton, indeed. Chewable? No. Soft-spoken? Very. But no yes-man. Contrarily to my Master, Sam was a diplomat. Don't get me wrong: neither a liar, nor a semantic acrobat. He knew how to speak his mind without offending others. Though cautious, he was no coward. Another reason why my Master liked him: Sam made him laugh. He was British, see? The accent! Hilarious, thought D. Neither least nor last, his discretion.

And kind: when my Master decided that I must also fly the flag and had my bushy tail dyed orangeish, Sam whispered:

'Don't worry, Pandora. In Renaissance days, this was called Venetian blonde. Look around: twenty-four-carat gold everywhere. Consider yourself flattered!'

Nice try. Resentful as I was to be tampered with but recalling the abuse thrown at my Master on TV, my mood mellowed. What's hair dye compared to those blazing insults such as 'Egomaniac buffoon. Amoral filibuster. Ostentatious parvenu. Epitome of the arrogance of the ignorant. Racist. Digitally dysfunctional. Alpha narcissist' – and so on.

In short, I switched to feeling sorry for him rather than for myself.

Sam, as usual, read my mind. We navigated on the same wavelength.

'Consider this,' he said in that soothing voice of his. 'Who'd call his property Oceano y Tacos if he despised the Latinos? Who'd buy Adnan Khashoggi's, a Saudi, yacht, if he really rejected Muslims, um?'

We both sighed. Sighs tinged with irony.

Mr D (Master to me), Sam explained, was a Janus turning his double face on most people.

He and I were the only ones allowed a glimpse of his vulnerable side. D trusted us completely, knowing we were not only devoted to him, but to each other.

'Now listen: whatever stunt is on our boss's mind – some sort of subterfuge, my guess – we must act in synchronicity.'

I licked Sam's hand. It's nice to be spoken to with respect. I adored him. Too bad he wasn't a dog … delectable frisson.

The same evening, I slithered into my Master's private office. A dismal sight. He was crouched over his gold-gilded desk. He had cut the telephone cables with scissors tossed on the floor. His iPod, iPhones, whatever these things are called, were smashed. I could smell his Coca-Cola laced with whisky. Whisky! The man never, ever, drank booze. His brother had died from the addiction.

What was I, Pandora, to do?

Should you not be aware of my name's origins, go google. (Nutshell: I'm given, then robbed of a box containing extreme emotions. Many are evil. By chance or fate, one of them cannot escape: *hope*.)

Was hope all D had left?

***

The following day, Sam and I ruminated on the pain of rejection. My master told us, with his typical finesse, to f*** off. Minutes later, also characteristically, he apologised.

'Here's the plan. Can't bear my life anymore. Wanna know how people would react if I were different. Who'd stand by me, if I were ... powerless. Who'd betray me. Who'd stand by me. I wanna see what's constantly kept hidden from me. Who'd dare to call me a plasma-screen cartoon character, talking in bubbles, looking me in the eye. Got it?'

Sam and I did. Sort of.

'Right. Here's the plan. I'll become blind. The ultimate proof of my lucidity!'

What??? Lucidity, in my Mater's case, was tantamount to delirium tremens.

'Sam, you'll arrange a phoney car crash. Pandora, you'll play the guide dog or whatever it's called. You'll have to pretend, to fake, to pretend and fake. As for me, pretence will allow me to unmask the pretenders.'

(His repeating everything could be unnerving. The rationale behind it: given the dismal comprehension of his forceful insights, only repetition achieved awareness. Unless he believed in what the French call *la méthode Coué*.

Go google again.)

'Understood?'

Just in case, I wagged my tail.

'Good. You're the nucleus of this scheme. I will remain commander-in-chief. Make no mistake about it, as primitive Texans say,' D snickered.

I too could read Sam's mind. The guy was not impressed. Not appalled either. On one hand, he mused that the stunt would not require major inventiveness. On the same, Sam, from the beginning, had intended to use the experience of working for D as a dynamo for his memoirs. Speechwriting for abrasive D had always represented, first and foremost, a prelude. Sam had literary talent. He knew it. This new folly would fan and fuel inspiration. Add an interesting twist to the tale. Adorn the narrative.

His second hand was busy thinking.

An outline of coming chapters curled up in his mind. He recalled a sentence from a book he had edited months earlier. 'To be invisible, you must be blind.' It had seemed silly at the time, but now... Who on earth was the author? Some Andrea?

To help understand the mimicking involved, Sam persuaded D to watch *Scent of a Woman* on a loop. It would prove tricky to prevent D from exclaiming 'Hou-ha' every two minutes, Al Pacino style, but OK .

After much rehearsal and briefing, the phony accident was staged.

I skip the details; unbridled press, etc. For once, D was delighted. He'd outfoxed the Fox channel, who not long ago had called him 'oafish'. They'd feel bad on top of sorry!

Anyway.

My Master, chairman and all, became officially blind.

III

What D had not quite grasped: the radical changes he had to abide by. From not grabbing a glass he wasn't supposed to see to not reacting to documents left lying around he wasn't supposed to read (but never did, being a post-literate, to put it politely), he had to learn a behaviour utterly out of character: self-control. To restrain his bombastic bravado. To feign dependence. To restrict the range of retaliation. Plus: addicted to screens, story of his life, he'd be forced to ignore them.

At first, Sam and I had many a good laugh.

But then D's fits of fury against the press spoilt our fun. Any media not directly under his control had always been the focus of D's wrath. When satirical, sardonic and often salacious comments were aired, Sam had to turn off the sound on some pretext or other, and I, to anticipate the smashing of the TV.

'Payback time!' he hollered.

Taking matters in his mocked hands, D decided to hold a press conference. Oh-woof. Not his forte.

My friend tried to infuse confidence.

'You're subtle, Pandora. Don't ever forget that your Master is a wolf but also a lamb. Infantile, if you prefer. Treat him as a child. If he raises his voice or his arm, gently pull him back. If all fails, bark in order to divert attention.'

I tilted a perplexed head.

'Yes you can!' he grinned.

Well. The event went as badly as expected. Actually, D enhanced the general perception of him, blind or not, being a bully. Also characteristically, he was idiotically pleased with himself thereafter.

'I fooled them again, didn't I?'

Sam kept his mouth shut. I opened mine, indicating a sympathetic dog-smile. At the same time, I couldn't help being reminded of pitbulls, whom I particularly dislike. Ugly beasts. Anyway, Yvette's *dîner* mercifully distracted me.

Yes! Yvette. D had entreated – entreated! – Yvette, the French cook who had adopted me as a puppy, to come back.

Why? you might diligently ask. Well. Aside from her gastronomic talents, more appreciated by Mrs D than by him, she had become a rather celebrated singer in some Parisian cabaret. Her hit: 'J'aurais vouluuuuue être un artiste.' Multilingual Sam had translated the lyrics. Now blind, wasn't D supposedly besotted with music?

Truth is, the song really got under his skin. And when I say really, I mean deeply. Smells don't lie.

My ears, also, vibrated listening to it.

> *J'ai du succès dans mes affaires*
> *J'ai du succès dans mes amours*
> *Je change souvent de secrétaire*
> *J'ai mon bureau en haut d'une tour*
> *J'ai ma résidence secondaire*
> *Dans tous les D's de la Terre*
> *Au fond je n'ai qu'un seul regret:*
> [choubida, chimpoum]
> *J'aurais voulu être un artiiiiste*
> *Pour pouvoir inventer ma viiiie!*
> [chim poum]

In essence. Fame and fortune do not provide what an artist

is blessed with or compensate for what an actor experiences: the freedom of a chameleon. Or perhaps, Sam explained, it is authenticity that gets lost in the midst of one's Circus Maximus. Consider this, Pandora: Nero burned half of Rome to build a stage on which he could perform – sing, dance, kill, you name it. The doors of the theatre were locked. Thousands of Romans died clambering over the walls. When ultimately condemned as a public enemy, Nero's last words were: *Qualis artifex pereo*!

I kept very quiet, indicating ardent interest.

'Meaning: "What an artist dies in me!"'

Another player busted on the scene: Sophie, a Duchess (as she would never let anyone forget) of mixed origins (which she conveniently forgot). Suffice it to say that she was incensed not to be addressed by her title in the all-too-democratic US of A.

D liked snobs. Aristocracy reminded him of nothing, but that was the beauty of it. The Countess was a dog trainer. Her proviso: a noble pedigree – such as I, Pandora, owned. On my vaccine passport the name Fiolili von der Kitz appeared in gothic script. Hey, how grand can you get?

She was good at her job. Amongst many things, I learnt to look absent-minded while multi-tasking. The idea? Act in a bimbo-doggedness way, in order to be ignored.

An example:

D, having acquired a (titanium) blind stick, pretended to stumble around. Once, the wind blew his iconic baseball cap away. Furious, he runs after it. Just as well for my lead: I manage to make him skid back with my weight. No easy task, as he was a massively big man. But even we dogs know that mind can triumph over matter.

Elsewhere, he almost pushes an ashtray away – cigarettes akin to chemical weapons in his mind. No, no, no! Or else he leaves his cane leaning against some chair and strides to pick it up; again, I intervene just in time.

Of course, the opaque eyeshades got on his nerves. Lawns looked ashen; the sky, always thunderstormy; his own kids … black. Black!

For credibility, Sam removed D's watch. What kept the latter from freaking out were acoustics. Interesting. Not used to it, he discovers that listening can serve both as a clock and a compass. He also becomes very attentive to smells. (As is well documented, the olfactory is one of the senses most atrophied in Homo so-called sapiens' evolution.)

My Master, seldom – if ever – fazed, was stunned.

The fake handicap revealed many hitherto unsuspected aspects of life.

Myriam, his spectacular wife, having done all that money can buy to look forever younger, gradually stopped wearing make-up or miniskirts. She looked happier than ever, D surreptitiously noticed. Their marriage had depended on appearance. She let go. Now, she could laugh without her jaw snapping as a result of too many liftings: loads of silicone had been removed. By way of compensation, she overdid the perfume bit: Poison by Dior. My Master and I suffered from sneezing fits. Why, by the way, are perfumes given names such as Poison, Opium, Witch or, can you believe it, Rogue?

Sam had also tossed mirrors aside to increase D's sense of disorientation. (I hate the things. Cannot forget when, as a puppy, I watched another dog nose-to-nose, which felt ice-cold and insipid, then ran around like a dervish… A fool.)

Myriam, at first not amused, soon stopped caring. 'What the hell?' she chipped with a newly acquired aloofness.

My Master, however, lost his cool. How was he to ascertain that his self-tanning cream was evenly sprayed or that excessive hairspray didn't clog his streaks?

Again, I prevented him from throwing a tantrum.

Permanent vigilance! Just as well that Yvette and Sam rewarded me with tasty tit-bits. The job was so exhausting I sometimes envied fluffy doll dogs. Hey! No responsibilities other than looking decorative.

Extremely tricky was the television situation. Not supposed to see images, D had to be prevented from reacting to them. Myriam – by now wearing flip-flops – muffled the noise with syrupy music. The desired effect was prompt to materialise: robbed of the constant background babble, D would skitter back to his suite, with me at the bow and all sorts of electronic devices on his desk.

Then, an administrative problem arose.

When blind, in the US, dark glasses and a white cane do not suffice. You need an armband. In order for it to be attributed, ophthalmological certificates are required.

Cash is king, this much we have established, but even D had to go through the motions.

Poor Sam. A decent and law-abiding man, he found himself in a quandary. To fool D's hypocritical profiteers was one thing. To lie to the authorities and cheat taxpayers, another. I could sniff his dilemma.

Thank Wolf, the Whoever-It-Was secretary was one of those bureaucratic viragos who believe a transcript represents the ultimate seal. She typed assiduously. Her superior, though mellifluous-faced with a wealthy man, was in a hurry. Neither of them noticed D shifting his chair to look over the ugly lady's shoulder. Glad not to be observed – or so she thought – her hair unwashed and her eyebrows unplucked, she too was in hurry: lunchtime! The guy gloated.

I sniffed his spite. D's reptilian mind *saw through* the man too. Understood! I authoritatively pulled on the leash, preventing my Master from lashing out in extremis.

Sam, the forever diplomat, displayed the sardonic courtesy the Brits are famous for, remarking on how the written word gains an authority of its own and praising the robotic secretary on her diligence. In the ensuing confusion, the signature at the bottom of the document was swift; case closed. D was now certified blind. And I, Pandora, his 'bodyguard'.

Yes, it simplified some matters, but not all.

Things were sour back at home. Yvette and Sophie hated each other's guts. Myriam hated both. 'A Faraday cage,' mumbled Sam. Though I didn't understand the words, I fathomed the meaning to have something to do with electrical tension.

Then: Pepita!

IV

One day, as we stroll on Fifth Avenue, a couple alights from its limousine.

'I know the bastard,' hushes D. 'Klem's been on the board forever. Shitty, syrupy, get the idea. What was Caesar's assassin called? Brutus, Brutal, Bruce? Point being, he's gotta dagger at hand to stab me in the back. Let's see!'

Whereupon he pretends to stumble over the suitcase the

driver has deposited on the sidewalk and convulses with pain.

The supposed bastard, recognising him, noticing the stick, the armband and the glasses, cannot hide his glee. So what he had heard on the news was accurate, for a change?

'Well, well. Whatever happened?'

'A car crash,' winces D.

'So very sorry,' the man beams.

Who helps D? Not the driver. Not the associate. Klem's wife. Shocked and shaking, she heaves heavy D up; produces a linen handkerchief to wipe his forehead; whispers consoling words and invites him inside to recover.

Pepita is so sweet, so genuine, so genuinely, sweetly kind that the impossible happens: D falls in love. Boom.

Love! He has known infatuation, mostly in terms of size zero and sexual kicks. Never in terms of character.

Pepita's face is moon-like. Her legs are hidden by boots; just as well. But her voice! Her joyousness! Everything about her is natural. It feels warm. Blatantly different from his antiseptic existence.

So reluctant is he to leave that he offers up a substantial piece of his real-estate cake – the very one the potential traitor has been craving. 'Rich is no four-letter word,' he adds, trying to amuse Pepita. She smiles, yes, but her heart isn't in it. When she gets D's name wrong, her husband scolds her. She blushes.

Too good to be true! thinks D: 'No idea as to who I am.'

I wag my tail in pendulum-circle-mode. Not easy. A rare occurrence, indicating euphoric enthusiasm: my Master was happy. Wow, Woof, Wolf, whatever. Strictly semantically speaking, it's called evidence (or so Sam, the loyal biographer-in-chief, whispered into my ear, showing yet again respect for my cognitive qualities).

'I've always avoided negative people,' snaps Klem, whom everybody else had forgotten. 'They have a problem for every solution.'

If the guy hoped to elicit laughter, he could dream again.

Diagonal talk ensued. Allowing myself a snooze, I dreamt of love. An apprenticeship, right? It's everywhere, all the time. Should be a duty to seize it.

Would The Boss be able to?

Pepita is moved. Her heart feels giddy. The exchange of silences makes the chemistry acutely perceptible – for me.

We leave.

'Sam,' says D in a husky voice. 'Find out everything you can about that babe. Asap.' He adds: 'Please,' then sinks into the most transparent of broodings.

***

In her Fifth Avenue boudoir, for the first time in a long time, Pepita examines herself. Tztz. She opens a drawer, retrieves lipstick, mascara, foundation – but no perfume. Allergic to the stuff.

Half an hour later, she looks transformed. Well; no movie star, but... In another drawer, she finds a diet guide, its pages yellowish. What's the point of slimming for a blind man? She dismisses the question.

Klem walks into the bathroom.

'What the f*** are you doing? A Halloween rehearsal?'

'A collage, dear!' she flutes back playfully.

'Women!' retorts her husband, slamming the door, clueless as to what a collage is. Carnage is the closest word he can think of.

Not wasting a moment is Sam's job.

Within the hour, he reports:

Pepita is of Argentinian origin. Her late father a successful painter. Her mother abandoned husband and child for a rubber baron no sooner had her daughter been born.

She was sent to a British boarding school, became used to a way of life riddled with laziness and complacency. Collages being her passion, she enrolled in the Chelsea Art School. No talent, she was told. Disheartened, she returned to Denver. Her father had remarried. She felt unwelcome, and was.

At a loss, she meets Karl Klem. A sugar daddy – not only money, but also gluttony-wise. Eating three dessert courses in Michelin-starred restaurants, plus devouring, then splitting up, businesses in order to sell the component parts and make more money to swallow more of the same, sums up his life.

Pepita becomes an over-fed, fed-up woman.

She is sad. But not knowing what she misses, having never experienced it, she waits for she is unsure what.

When D trips over her suitcase, she has just turned forty. In fact, it's her birthday.

Karl, having flown her to Paris in order to have a feast at Maxim's, the cherry on the cake a multi-carat emerald brooch, considers that he's done his bit. He now lies in bed, thinking of D.

Was his offer serious? Had the psychopath, now blind, become bland? During their last board-meeting, he had delivered predictable streams of invectives and incendiary diatribes; harped on about the system's weakness – adding he'd redistribute, re-evaluate, god-not-what-else the value of his company to benefit the under-privileged. 'Ha! That's rich coming from a billionaire given a million dollars as pocket money aged twenty!' Klem had fumed. Cash might be king, he snorted, but time is my personal army. Pleased with his formula, Klem had lit a fat cigar and blown the heavy smoke right into The Chairman's face. Predictably, the self-proclaimed billionaire had fled, his aversion to tobacco even more violent than to perfume.

But Klem's indignation did not abate. Quite the reverse.

The perfidious double-crosser could not, possibly, believe he took his proposition at face value, could he? Would he, Klem, not the most subtle of negotiators, granted, but still, fall for that kind of shit? Be fooled by D, of all consistently inconsistent clowns? Whose only reality was transactional – when in his favour, of course? By D, the same who had bankrupted small businesses withholding pay on the grounds of quality shortcomings? Who had inflated his personal wealth whilst betraying and often suing his cronies – profiting from corporate mega-debts? Whom US banks would no longer lend a cent? Ha.

Trust the very D who, asked for $5,000 by his former school, had waved a forged one-million-dollar bill before tossing a meagre $200 into the principal's pocket? Vicious! D, the xenophobic haranguer who hired and fired illegal Polish workers hours before attending charity venues. C'mon!

Here, Klem had to scurry for his asthma spray.

No relief whatsoever. Notwithstanding a large brandy, his rage reignited with a vengeance.

D as in Dealer, trading favours when not bribes? With an attention span of two hundred symbols and twenty seconds? Presenting him with a deal? That scoundrel oozing sudden goodwill? Talking about…

Where was his wife?

While these mental sparks were erupting on Fifth Avenue, Sam worked in his five-square-metre office.

Hacking around, he recaptured emails Pepita had sent to girlfriends. Resumé: she missed England. Art. Freedom. She often wept. She had only just subscribed to Weight Watchers and Viennese Waltz classes.

The very next morning, D's tailor fit him with tweeds. A technician programmed channels retransmitting cricket and snooker, instantly installed in his bathroom's TV. A gardener had been instructed to reproduce Blenheim Palace's rose nursery.

'Bright Head Revisited,' chuckled Sam.

I erected my ears into question marks. Sam's train of thought wasn't always easy to catch.

Giving so many orders, D sounded like he'd lose his voice. A dogging prospect: blind, oh well; but mute on top? I trailed him to bed. Sam had dissolved a Stilnox 20 into his evening milkshake. The man needed to calm down.

We returned downstairs.

There, another unexpected development was awaiting us.

Myriam, my Master's wife and trophy, stood at the bottom of the stairs in a mini-monokini.

'Sam,' she cooed, 'let's go for a swim. You must be dead. I've prepared caviar blinis. Oscietra. Staff given the night off.'

In spite of the haze (other than candles all over the place, it was really dark) I saw bottles in silver buckets, and heard some sort of hypnotic music. Weird mist made me squint.

Humans! I hurried back to my basket in the kitchen.

Next to it, a steak cut in thin slices. To ensure omertà?

Bribe or not, I savoured both supper and slumber. Didn't even need to count sheep.

V

The next two days were, thank Wolf, uneventful. D and his wife had flown to the Cayman Islands 'to open the post', as they would put it. Sam hardly ever emerged from his bedroom, probably having a well-deserved rest. I ambled around leisurely, enjoying not being on a lead.

On the third, a Wednesday (lamb cutlets), I became worried. Still no sign of my friend Sam. Breaking my pledge of utmost discretion, I pawed his door open – and yelped in shock.

Sheets on the floor, breathing spasmodically, his body was hard to distinguish on the white mattress, such was his paleness. I licked his hand, barked melodiously; all to no avail. Panicking, I rushed downstairs four at a time. Yvette immediately understood.

An hour later, shaved and showered, Sam lay on crisp linen. He even accepted something to eat – then had to throw up.

Myriam had left drastic orders: no communication whatsoever until their return.

What were we to do?

'Maybe just nerves,' speculated Yvette.

Had something traumatic happened by the pool the night D passed out?

I had heard on some TV programme that certain events can cause a catatonic state – a complicated word, I know, but explained with great patience by some sort of teacher, who had added: in a first phase, the afflicted person sinks into an opaque silence. Indeed, my voluble friend would not utter a word.

Resolving to trigger phase number two, I bit his ankle. Gently ... but still. That, I think, made Sam snap out of his torpor.

Things moved swiftly from there on.

Sam admitted he was ill but insisted he'd allow only one physician in the whole entire world to examine him: Doctor Tony from London, a forever friend of his. Calls were made by Yvette. A plane ticket organised. On Sunday, the Doc appeared.

A sight as astounding as the odour: the latter, rather vile. From what I could gather, the doctor had donned a bathrobe over pyjama trousers. He wore one leather shoe, one terry-cloth slipper. No luggage, other than a plastic bag in which bottles clinked.

'Toodeloo,' he bowed, kissing saucer-eyed Yvette's hand before stroking my head with utmost gentleness.

We liked him instantly.

'May I, *si vous le permettez*, ask whether you had a little ... *contretemps?*'

The mirrors in the hall having been removed, and the doctor not altogether sober, it took him a moment to realise the allusion to his appearance. He keeled over laughing.

'A refreshment in the size and shape of a large gin and tonic? On an armchair, perhaps?'

'*Avec Plaisir*,' said Yvette, all trace of her usual severity evaporated.

She led him onto the veranda. Had I been gifted with telepathy, I'd have known the Doc reminded her of Dudley Moore in the film *Arthur*; a cult film in that it also reminded her of her most ardent flirtation, many eclipses ago… Yvette, in turn, reminded the Doc of one of his flings, Aleana something or other.

In any event: the medical eminence from London and the French cook hit it off. When he told her about his transit night in Miami, she wobbled in mirth.

'In that Hilton or Hyatt, what's the difference, I head straight to the outdoor bar. Almost ten hours without smoking! Well. There, I meet this most maaorvellous lady – well, forget the lady bit, let's call a hooker a hooker. The price of the pleasure of her company negotiated, we have a maaorvellous time downtown. A night-cap in my abode included in the transaction, we do what bees do (hums a melody) without the love bite, as far as I recall. Fact is, I recall pretty little, other than waking up, the shoe in which I had taken the astute precaution of stashing my cash was gone, as was my suitcase. Just as well I had left passport and credit cards in the coded safe,' he concluded merrily.

His good humour contagious, I rolled to and fro on the carpet.

'Right oh,' the Doc said, suddenly erect as a candle. 'Where's the patient?'

Shame on me. In all the commotion, I had forgotten him. My tail at half-mast, I headed for Sam's bedroom.

Merely by touching him, as softly as he had my head, the diagnosis was delivered adamantly: diverticulitis but also something else.

'The man is psychosomatically dispirited. Has he suffered some sort of shock? His reflexes are delayed. He acts guilt-ridden…'

Yvette raised her eyebrows heavenwards. 'No idea.'

I had several, but neither willing nor capable of sharing them, I curled into a corner.

How come the English word 'dumb' both means stupid and speechless? Totally unfair.

VI

All of us in a meditative mood, we jumped upon hearing a car screech to a halt and, seconds later, the entrance door slam.

Mr and Mrs D were back.

Tony knew a thing or too many about the man, none eliciting admiration. Improbably, however, my Master and Tony bonded – the former well aware that his blindness act hadn't fooled the Doc for a second, whatever the amount of the incentive.

Myriam declared she'd go to see Sam.

'You will not!'

The Doc's tone pre-empted protest. Even D was taken aback. His wife, vexed and not just a little, retreated.

'Bitch,' boomed my Master. 'Of course she doesn't see me notice how she undulates around every young man in sight, or practises forging my signature in front of my very own, wide-shut eyes.' Here he snorted. 'I recommend the trick. Astounding what you find out. Now, my friend, do me a favour: ask that French gal for a treble whisky. Half of it will go into my Coke, OK ?'

'Sure thing,' replied Tony, parodying his host's accent and rather pleased with the arrangement.

Half an hour later, drunk as a skunk, D had poured out his heart. Pepita. Couldn't forget her. Had drafted many letters whilst locked in his bathroom, but happy with none. The lady having been raised in the UK, less United by the day, but that was beside the point; could Tony help him with the finishing touches?

'Polishing your prose?'

'Ha. See? Words! By the way, I'll get my driver to buy you shoes and all the rest, man.'

He chuckles. The kids department in Bloomingdale will do. But what the Doc lacks in stature, he makes up in terms of smartness. D likes and fears that in equal measure.

Measurements taken, D retrieved a crumpled paper from his back pocket.

'Wrap your eyes around this,' he commanded.

Hi pretty woman,

Can't get you out of my fucking mind. Wanna make u life great again. Wanna make you free and mine. Ain't a poet but heard about the language of flowers so I buy a chain of shops selling the stuff. Your hub needn't know where they come from. Let him think they're for him for all I care. Blind I am, but a colour-code there is: they'll be red. Passion and all that. Watch bottom of the vases.Something shiny down there. Why I think of u all the time? Cause you're natural. I'm surrounded by artificial. Make-believe, get my drift? Pepita, I need to see – nah, honey, hear – you again. I forbid you to ask Karl for info about me. It's mostly rumours and bad, bad things written by not smart people who wanna harm me out of envy. Let's go to a hotel I don't own, babe, I just mean, let's be alone somewhere. My instincts are always right and they tell me we can be proud together.

Call. My number is [...]. Early in the morning best. Love, money, whatever you want.

Goodness me, muses Tony. Pretty Woman? Tricky. What Julia Roberts's profession was is known. Then: a love letter dictating behaviour? Please. Yet, D's maladroitness is touching. But then again. To call a perfect stranger *honey*? Honestly. How could a man writing such crap ever have acquired power? Isn't power based on the subtleties of persuasion? Lastly, his letter was a succession of I's and Me's. He suspected Pepita got enough of that at home.

'Why don't you get Sam to fix this? Isn't he your confidant?'

'Con-what?'

'Right-hand man, sir.'

'But I'm not a leftie! And some secrets must be held secret, with many leaks and things, believe me.'

Enchanted with his repartee, D had more whisky wheeled in. Fair enough, thought the Doc. Putting pencil to paper, he drafted:

Fair Lady dearest.

My mind has been swirling ~~with your image~~ around you ever since our first encounter. My most ardent desire is to make you ~~happy and mine~~ joyful and fulfilled. You need to fly; I need to be grounded. We need each other. It would, of course, be uncouth for a blind man to offer horizons; yet, delving deep into my inner self ~~sight~~, I am suffused with tender hope. Where the language of flowers resonates. Permit me to send you red bouquets every day (red, they say, the colour of passion). ~~Knowing Karl, he probably won't notice, in any case not question its provenance.~~ Karl might not even notice. Not even notice the sparkle that may shine among the stems...

You see, Pepita, my life is a sum of artifices. Some call it a scam: horrible people. It's all work for me. No fire – no warmth ... which is why I just cannot forget you.

Also why I entreat you not to attach importance to anything

you might read, or be ~~told about me. Rumours, by definition,~~ ~~are ill-informed and speculative.~~ May I further ask we meet somewhere private? My loss of sight – *not* foresight! – has made me allergic to crowds. I'm merely asking for a few moments of harmony. Please reply soonest. My very private number is—. Better after dinner, when the weight of responsibilities is somewhat lifted.

Prepared to love you to bits, were ~~it to entail falling~~ I to break into pieces, ~~my dreams chapped~~, I am and will remain
Yours Truly.

D threw violent abuse at him.

'What the hell you talking about? You some shake-pea or something? How's the gal supposed to understand what even I caint?'

The Doc shrugged.

'Let me check with Sam. I'm sure he'll make a better job of it. After all it's his.'

'His fucking what?' fumed D.

'Job.'

I could have ululated with indignation. That nice man, having travelled from the other side of the pond, as people say – thinking for the umpteenth time that only we who skip about know about the size of ponds – treated like a lackey! Not even thanked for his literary efforts? Dismissed without ado? I half-expected some heated argument. It didn't come forth. Pleased to return to his chain-smoking, exit the Doc. Enters Sam, swaying a little from all the medication. From my horizontal point of view: never a dull moment. Nice.

'I seem to have heard a trifle of disagreement down here. Could I…'

'A what? A rifle? Shit, can nobody talk normally in this house anymore?'

After a pause, one of D's mood swings sets in.

'You look like shit. What would you like, buddy?'

'Cornflakes.'

D slaps his hands.

'Here's my boy! D'you know I mounted a hostile take-over of KelloDs the other day?'

All sorts of cereals later my Master, as he would, returns to what most concerns him – until it wouldn't anymore, normally soon thereafter, the goal reached, the challenge ticked off.

'Your doctor, nice guy by the way, transformed my letter to Pepita into some sort of poem. She a Pulitzer Prize or some IQ queen? Rewrite. Make it snappy.'

Sam, not in the least surprised by the first version, nor by the elegant version of the second, plus longing to go back to bed, scribbles:

Dear, darling Pepita.

Impossible to chase you from my mind.

Warm and genuine, you are unforgettable.

I need you and you need me. We need each other.

You are my sun, and I am your star. [D liked that, though he'd have preferred Superstar, but OK .]

The language of flowers says it all. Especially when the stems hide a gem. Have a look. I can't. Yet I feel sparkle when I think of you. Will enjoy peace, at long last, if we meet somewhere peaceful. Call me soonest. I entreat you – not in my habits. My cell—

Jumping to his feet, D exclaimed:

'I like that! You're the best! It's almost a tweet!'

Sam didn't even feel insulted. The man had no inkling as to the difference between a twit and a tweet.

VII

At this unfortunate point, Myriam stumbles in. The dope her masseur had been paid to make her smoke hasn't done the trick of numbing her until the following day – the very day when D expects his business hero Algernon Duff. Possibly the only entrepreneur he respects.

Well aware that the reverence isn't reciprocated, D paces from porch to pool.

The groggy wife, meanwhile, tries to coax Sam into the kind of conversations men hate, on the lines of honesty, feelings, consequences and intentions.

D stomps back into the house and shouts:

'Waste of time, you silly woman. He'll never get mixed up with you. Get yourself a new gardener. I need Sam – now! We have to prepare tomorrow's meeting with that Brit, right?'

Toxic or not, I inhale the smoke rising from the fireplace Mrs D keeps firing up, probably hoping her husband will retreat to his air-conditioned abodes; most improbable, as contaminating the surroundings is the least of his concerns. Ashes swirl all over the marble floor. I must be the only one in this house not obliged to wear plastic wraps around his feet, well, my paws, like in hospitals.

'Play it again, Sam.'

'What?'

'The record from the other day. About Brit manners, habits and all that stuff.'

'Aaaaargh. That. All rightie.'

'No nursery language with me. Get on with it!'

I distractedly listened to my friend's lecture, expecting to doze off, but the corners of my muzzle turned upwards.

As the attentive reader may have noticed, I share some unusual traits with two-leggers. Apart from the unusual scope of my vocabulary: a sense of irony.

Sam's briefing:

'Look here, boss. Mr Duff, other than being an oil tycoon and an art collector, is known for his wicked wit. He and the Doc, by the by, have...'

'By the how much?'

'By chance. As I was saying, they are quite good friends.'

D's impatience grew unmitigated.

'To the point, man.'

'Getting there.'

I could hear an undertone of amusement in his voice. Sam was enjoying D's fretting.

'Here goes. Thanks to the Pepita episode, you have the ultimate elegant wardrobe...'

Oh Wolf! At the mention of her name, D recoils. She has not answered his letter.

'Please concentrate. So in terms of dress code, all is well. Now, the manners: etiquette would require you to...'

'Skip that bit. Call it a brand. Mine.'

'Right. Now, the essential bit. Self-deprecation.'

'What?' D barked.

'Basically you have to – well, pretend to – disparage and belittle yourself or your achievements, see? From the Latin, deprecate, meaning...'

'Whaddya mean? How I am supposed to do *that*? And as to Latin, let me tell a thing or two about the biggest crooks of all! The Vatican bankers, worse than any Capone & Co...'

I slithered to my Master's feet and nibbled at his socks. Wasn't my job to keep his temper and divagations in check?

'Look,' Sam continued, grateful for my manoeuvre. 'Take the expression: too clever by half. In the US a compliment, in England an insult. Understate your intelligence.'

'My...?'

'Yes. Sorry. Might not come easy, but most efficient.'

Finally, a word D could identify with. Sam gave up on explaining the difference between French esprit, based on double entendres, misogyny and culture, and English harmless wit.

'Let's put it like that: you must never seem to take anything seriously. You must seem to worry more about Pandora than about money. You must claim that all the gold around you is plated. Mr Duff will have seen at first glance that it is not, and will appreciate your false modesty. The more absurd the things you say, the better. That's what we call conversation, see?'

Pacing the vast drawing room, D groaned. Conversation, to him, was an exchange of information; preferably with a hamburger on his plate and a fat profit at arm's length. A meal was to last precisely forty-five minutes. Beating around the bush, horrible name, not his style.

'All this crap necessary?'

'If you want to display the "Art of The Deal" with an old-school Brit, I'm afraid so.'

Sam pondered. D tapped away on his calculator.

'Boss, I've had an idea: Duff wants land to drill oil. You hardly need more of it, do you? Oil not in your line of business, why not ask him ... for the Chelsea Art School in return? In exchange? Get my drift?'

Daft or not, D was fast when impatient. Sam now held his undivided attention.

'A.D., as Duff is called, commands much influence in London's art world. Pepita seems to care for that more than for jewels...'

'Got it. Next.'

'You might also contemplate down-tuning your high profile. In England, celebrity is considered somewhat ... vulgar.'

Sam refrained from adding ostentation to fame and D, from telling him to shut the fuck up.

'One last thing. An English gentleman is never taken aback. He's laid-back. And no politics! Normally, throwing in a mention of Ascot is an icebreaker. In Duff's case, however, better mention Venice. He loves the place – Venice in Italy, that is... Here's a book I took the liberty of purchasing. Pictures only, worry not.'

VIII

While this conversation was taking place, Algernon Duff was being driven from Miami airport to D's estate in Palm Beach. He didn't look forward to a negotiation that might turn into a confrontation with a famously serpentine-brained character. But he needed that land! Like all tycoons, skirting taxes marinated at the bottom of his mind.

The meeting encapsulated an experience Duff would henceforth delightfully mimic in his St James's Club.

He was steered straight to the pool house. 'My office's being renovated,' claimed his host. Duff knew better: it would be lined with photographs of the man and his sycophants; encumbered with glossy magazines depicting D on its cover; golf trophies and what not.

Whereupon a vintage port was wheeled in – aside an apple-crumble pie! D wore knickerbockers. Had he envisaged a kilt? Algernon had trouble not chuckling aloud.

The good news: he obviously was keen to make a deal.

The dodgy question: what sort?

When D started raving about Venice ('So much water! I love water! So many boats! I love boats!') Duff laughed heartily. This flattered his host.

To cut a long story short: all the billionaire had wanted in exchange for a piece of land whose value he no doubt had had assessed ... was the rather moribund Chelsea Art School. Duff couldn't believe it. Especially when D added he would by no means interfere with its running, apart from injecting cash. 'It's a present for a lady, er...' (Manly wink.)

Astounding, again. So the man, that man, had a crush on some girl. Not a stripper or a model; an artist! Blimey!

I held up my head regally in acquiescence, enjoying the sniff of Mr Duff's trousers. They whiffed of faraway heather.

The necessary documents were prepared, or rather printed out in what seemed split seconds, which suited Algernon fine, having nil desire to linger. Whereupon an unmistakable silhouette stumbled to the table.

Tony the Doc! What was this nutcase doing there?

'Hullo Alg,' he managed to articulate. 'Isn't that spllllendid?'

'Go get the Nokia OZO, hell no, the LucidCam VR made in America!' D barked at the nearest bodyguard. 'A meeting of 3Ds!'

The two Englishmen were openly laughing as they were

filmed flanking him; they looked like Lucky Luke's three Daltons. A piece of anthology!

Algernon Duff departed.

'Pandora,' whispered ever tender-hearted Sam, 'don't be sad. He might be back. I know, I know,' he added, fondling my drooping neck, 'you fell for AD. Oh well. I'm sure he'll send a bone one of these days.'

The power of magical thinking. He did. From Fortnum & Mason!

IX

Days later, my Master received the long-awaited call in his study, loudspeaker on.

Pepita was touched. She agreed to meet him but would D please come to her place? She wasn't 'the hotel kind of woman'. Her husband was travelling.

'Would you mind?' she girlishly pleaded.

When he crossed the threshold, with me conspicuously guiding his steps, his first reaction was shock. Marble and gold everywhere, a majestic staircase, no books or ash-trays: the Bad Guy had reproduced his, D's, style, to the minutest detail, since he had last been there. Smug creep! Outrageous.

His second reaction was one of further shock.

Pepita had slimmed herself into an almost androgynous shape. She wore make-up and red stilettos.

'Let's go to my abode, shall we?' she murmured.

Abode?

Turned out she had a flat within the flat. It was filled with canvasses, kilims, the walls painted a warm ochre.

'I understand you like Coke Light. With lemon?' He

had, yes, digitally affirmed that 'thin people don't drink Diet Coke,' but how the hell was she to know?

D's mood, I could sense, became sombre. He longed for Sam to give him a clue as to what to say, or a clue as to what to do. On impulse, he walked straight towards the sofa before I could pretend to lead the way. Woof almighty. But Pepita (belief perseverance and so on) didn't notice.

She brought some cushions, 'should your back ache'. She brought a gift-wrapped box; in it, a Swiss cuckoo clock, 'so you'll hear what time it is, at least every quarter of an hour.' She did not wear the diamond watch he had Tiffany's put at the bottom of a rose-filled vase. No flowers in sight either.

But then … she interrupted her comings and goings to ask whether he would be offended if, in terms of dinner, she presented meatballs: 'Not very refined, I know, but a craving of mine.'

D's spirits lit up instantly. They talked. He about himself; she about herself. A vivid, exclusive interest in their mutual spheres seemed to forge a bond. Both had forgotten thirsty me. Leaving the couple to their criss-crossing monologues, I wiggled into the kitchen, managed to open the tap standing on my back legs, and gulped some water, at last. To my delight, Pepita had thought of me after all. There was a plate with another hamburger on the floor. Nice lady.

When I slithered back, they both lay on the sofa. Sleeping. At opposite corners. Well! Not that I'm an expert, but it didn't much whiff of ardent passion.

Finally I barked. It was getting black and Sam had given instructions. Mrs D was hosting some ambassador or other.

My Master grudgingly got to his feet.

'Ok, Pandora, OK . You're right. Good Dog…'

Pepita yawned then sprung up.

'I'm so sorry! It's all this weight loss. I feel weak all the time. I do apologise, darling D!'

Weak? Good: he'd protect her and also ask her to get a little plump again. Apologise? Good: guilt means leverage. The darling bit? Couldn't she speak Americana?

'Wanna know the truth, babe? Haven't slept well for ages. Thanks. My present today? The Chelsea Art School.'

He handed her the property's deeds.

'Can't believe it,' she stuttered, the smell of perplexity – mingled with outrage – pungent.

'Do. It's all yours. By the way, where are the roses?'

'They're all over the place,' she joyfully lied.

'Really? In any case, tomorrow, same time, at my Plizza hotel. Got it?'

She did. All in all, D was ghastly.

Why did he dress like a B-movie rip-off of a Sherlock Holmes spoof; then his manners, as graceful as a mob boss's; and also, that trill from the mobile phone: '*If I Were a Rich Man, dadadilalaladidilalalaptralala...*' Goodness me! Pepita never appeared on the following day. Her chauffeur did, envelope in hand. In it, the diamond watch and a laconic note:

'Sorry darling. Off to London. Off to pursue my passion. You saved my life. Careful with yours. Husband plotting assassination. Takeover scheme. P.'

My Master called Sam in a fury.

'You know what to do, man. Find out everything – and I mean every fucking thing about that bastard Klem's whereabouts, phone calls and all that jazz. NOW!'

Had I been smaller, I would have crawled underneath some piece of furniture. D's irascible character, when at its pitch, was terrifying. As we left the hotel for the heliport, I must have looked like a water skier towed by a speedboat.

Sam found out a lot, but only the FBI, whom D loathed, came up with the whole story.

D was to hold a press conference two days later announcing his commitment to the Arts, his purchase of..., just the first step in a massive philanthropic endeavour, etc.

Klem, knowing that D's only weak spot was children, had hired a professional killer in the form and shape of a dwarf. The latter was to be perched on the shoulders of one of his tallest henchmen, made to look like a kid (exempted from body search) holding a pink plastic camera into which a gun was fitted. This, in turn, would pass security, whose metal detection devices were no higher than 6'6" Conclusion:

D cancelled the event. Klem fled to Mexico, where he was killed by a drug lord on my Master's payroll. The Chelsea Art School deeds were reverted, this time for good, into Sam's name. Pepita bought them back (and would later become famous, not only for her exhibitions but for her exhibitionism, having moulded herself into a cunning courtesan).

My loyal friend and I are presented with prime Japanese Kobe beef.

Woof.

X

To have Sam to herself became an obsession. He'd been, albeit unwillingly, even half-unconsciously, her best lover for years. Forget it? No way. She was Mrs D after all, a born Donawittch.

Myriam had double agents of her own. 'People who know how to wait,' she'd hiss. She knew all about the Pepita episode. 'Might leaking it to the media accelerate my husband dearest's downfall from grace? Not sure. Shareholders, by now, are past caring about his caprices. Reveal the Cayman Islands arrangement? Nah.'

Concretely, there was the far-from-trivial issue of the pre-nup agreement. Should she be identified as the string-puller, she'd cut the grass from under her feet. Not an option. Sam was penniless.

She was aware of having caused him distress. His manner had become clumsy, his glances evading. He, for one, was a man of integrity. To deceive his boss once more would cause a moral dilemma bound to cause more illness, meaning, Myriam shuddered, impotence. Not the idea. Persuade the guy that her husband would drop him as soon as he was considered redundant? Again: how to proceed?

A bit of misinformation channelled through, hmm, Yvette for instance, or that brain-dead Labrador might do the trick. The seeds of distrust already planted by D's disenchanted entourage only needed to be fertilised; but how? Hmm again. A tape reproducing fabricated tapping of Sam's cell phone? Would that suffice? Not sure. D knew all the tricks, having used them against his opponents time and again.

Concentration is the essence, she reminded herself, reclining on the sofa of the smallest salon among a myriad of others – the only one she could called hers, pink and mauve and cosy. Myriam swept her martini aside.

Objective no.1: Sam. Seduce and conquer. In order to, etc.

Objective no.2: discredit D enough to secure an

advantageous divorce. In order to, etc.

Objective no.3: Plant...

'Since when do you write?' a thunderous voice boomed.

D, towering above her, looked like a massive pumpkin. Probably overdosed on the self-tanning cream.

Myriam stuttered, 'just a list of things to do, you know...'

'Like manicure, ladies' lunches, shopping for toy boys?'

'Darling dearest, you're unfair!' she squealed.

It worked. D jumped.

'What kinda word is that?'

'Wouldn't you like to know, darling? And by the way, I wasn't writing, I was drawing, see? A sudden interest in arts, like...'

Myriam stopped. Sharp.

How on earth did D know she'd been sitting with pad and pencil in her hands? Come to think of it, where was Pandora? The door had been closed but he hadn't collided with it.

A suspicion sneaked into, then invaded, her mind. Gucci Almighty! All of it a hoax? Her first reaction: to comb her hair with her fingers and hide her un-pedicured feet. The second, a eureka of sorts: 'Gottya!'

And so she did. Having tested and trapped D in various ways or situations, it was *wow* certain: her husband's blindness was feigned. He had fooled her and everyone else. Bad enough – had Sam not been his presumed accomplice. Smug son of a bitch. Now she understood the role of that haughty, dog-training Duchess. As to Pandora! A real bitch, that dog had displayed talents worthy of The Actor's Studio.

The flip side was the sunny one: she, Myriam, had all and more she needed to blackmail the bastards. D into a costly divorce; Sam into sexual slavery. He'd ultimately love her. This called for a double martini. Why not two?

XI

What followed was nasty. Tasted of rotten meat and smelled likewise.

Mrs D had bribed one of her lovers into filming my Master's every missteps with the so-called LucidCam VR.

D, unmasked, retreated into his suite and would let no one in, except lawyers. Food trays were deposited in front of the door.

I missed the Doc, who'd been sent packing.

I missed Yvette even more. Ditto.

Sam and I were put in a quarantine of sorts. He started writing with furore, then with gusto (his words).

'A Trap into Which He Willingly Fell' was his book title.

But me? Idleness was torture. I had no one to do nothing with. The new cook, an expert with vegetarian biological food, was a homosexual who hated animals. An animal! I'd never been called that before. As to Mrs D? She had the whole place repainted in pastel colours. Very disorientating as shiny gold had provided me with useful landmarks, so to bark.

I too started to lose weight and, feeling weak, now understood Pepita better. Bored, I felt useless. As two-leggers would say, I sank into depression. Routine having been abolished, time was tricky to track.

And then, once upon a day or another, my Master erupted from his seclusion.

'Pandora you sexy beast! Go get Sam! We got things to do!'

He tickled my neck. The sun shone again.

Not for long.

Emaciated, D found it hard to swallow 'the vandalism' of his iconic HQ. Turned from a sultan's palace to a doll's house! Photographers and TV crews now camped outside. Shutters were drawn day and night. Myriam, triumphant, hands on wide hips, basked in her soon-to-be ex's disarray.

His seclusion had triggered off much speculation, none favourable to THE WORLD Ltd.'s stock-price value. Rumours as to his stunt had spread like a bond-fire – naturally fuelled by Mrs D's lawyer, the voracious Hollywood shark confusingly called Marlin Tender. Oftentimes compared with Machiavelli, he'd point out that the Florentine author of *The Prince* had always been an arch-pragmatist, hence 'the ends justify the means' adage. Should it entail devastation, so be it.

All of that and much more I know because Sam had fallen into the habit of reading whatever he wrote aloud 'to check the music'. Quite a lot I also forget. A healthy mind is good at defragmentation. You need to delete in order to make space for new memories – and Wolf knows that in my Master's surroundings, one needed it. Befuddling developments lurked around every corner.

Take Mrs D.

Her none-too-subtle overtures led nowhere. Sam would send back the bottles of Château Lafite untouched. Same with Turnbull & Asser shirts or P.G. Wodehouse leather-bound first editions. Seduction in the flesh was equally ignored. Transparent kaftans; shoulder-high leather gloves; lenses that transformed her already lapis lazuli eyes into emeralds: all to no avail. He kept his bedroom locked at night – with me by his side. Already a guide dog (at least in public, as at home it had become nonsensical) during the day, I morphed into a ferocious watchdog at night. Useful again! Bliss.

Not least, Yvette was back! My Master had regained the upper hand.

Yes. He was a fireball of energy. 'Best defence is attack,' was his ad nauseam reiterated harangue. (Four words! A feat.)

In that spirit, D now planned a historic conference: a gathering of major shareholders, even the calamitous media or foreign investors. Time to cast the net wide.

Sam and I were not privy to the frenzy of preparation. Believing in partitions and walls, D's staff meetings in his vast offices were off-limits to us. Just as well. My friend, of course, was totally absorbed in the writing of D's speech for the occasion. And I, by watching over him.

I could sense his unease.

He scribbled down Machiavelli's phrase, 'conspiracies are misguided because, if they fail, the intended victim always rises to greater power and many times from being a good man, becomes vicious.' Good vs. Bad sounded like D, no doubt about that, but ... a double-edged interpretation was risky. Better disseminate lukewarm information and vague decisions in a conciliatory tone. His draft:

As the Chairman of a self-founded company called THE WORLD, I call for everybody to rally to far- and clear-sighted, long-term goals – and yes, my blindness had been real but Thank The Lord, only temporary. No, I haven't misled anyone! What I have is gained an all-encompassing sense of perspective. It was, truth be told to power and vice versa, a miracle! [Here a pregnant pause, followed by an appeal to brotherly kinship.]

Divorce! Don't we all how bad a divorce can get? Soon I'll be accused of having mistreated Pandora, my beloved Pandora! [Another pause to keep the audience breathlessly guessing.] My faithful Dog! [Here, an applause-permitting pause.]

Sam burst into sardonic laughter.

'The worst speech I ever wrote,' he hiccoughed. 'Bah. It'll fulfil the purpose of arresting attention, if only for being incomprehensible, i.e. incongruous. Let me follow along these lies – oops! Lines was what I meant...'

I wiggled my tail euphorically. To be mentioned by name in my Master's ground-breaking speech! How honoured can a Labrador Lady get?

'Right,' pursued Sam. 'Let's toss in things like, I don't only propose, I dispose; why bore you with the minutia of details, if all that counts are the results – and more of the same. D the showman will, as usual, count on the resonating and hypnotic effect of endless loops. Who in his right mind still expects some semblance of a link between cause and effect? A remnant of logic, if you will?'

I tried to shrug with suitable dog-may-careness, but my anatomy made it difficult.

Pandemonium indicated the date approaching.

Other than his usual tweets, my Master had sent gold-embossed invitations to the VIPs and (hitherto insulted) mainstream TV bosses and press barons.

The Plizza's ballroom would stage the event. About nine thousand chairs had been placed in geometric configurations. The platform had been lined with huge American flags and even bigger ones depicting D's initials. Acoustics were fine-tuned. A buffet abounding with Max D's hamburgers, Coke Light and Korean wine was laid out.

D waited a strategic ten minutes after the hour before bursting onto the scene. 'Let them fret.'

The shock! The stupefaction! The vexation!

What my Master saw made him choke. Cameras? Few and far between, none of them of impressive size. They directed their focus, viciously, on spots where one could discern the carpet in between sparsely occupied chairs. It created patches of barren, desert-like appearance. Where were his Foxy yes-crews?

D had been boycotted. Not only by the mainstream media: even by provincial networks. Shareholders? Not a single one wearing black tie, as had been stipulated on the invitations.

Behind the nearby curtain, I crawled into a ball. The pain felt like serrated metal around my neck. Sam lit a cigarette: a rare and utterly forbidden course of action. To top it all, there was a power cut. Accident or sabotage? Did it matter at this point?

No.

D had frozen into a statue. In a flash, I imagined Mrs D having a hearty laugh. Or the bullied staff drafting letters of resignation... (Useless. They'd be fired long before.)

Back to base, an excruciatingly long while later, D slammed the door of his private quarters.

We heard his white titanium cane thrown onto the veranda. Followed by his emblematic red cap. Soon thereafter, by the plasma TV screen he must have ripped off the wall.

Then? Nothing.

For a whole week.

During which, Wolf forbid, I snapped at Mrs D's ankle. Hard. She was packing up paintings which my Master *really* liked. No expert on divorces, as you can imagine, but there's a limit. Sam emerged from his torpor.

'Myriam dearest, I dare hope you're vaccinated against rabies!'

'Against what?'

'Rabies. A disease dog bites carry. Lethal. More than tetanus, equally deadly, which you surely have been…'

She turned various shades before running out.

Sam and I looked at each other, smiling our respective ways.

Our fleeting mirth was abruptly interrupted by D's appearance halfway down the stairs.

'Sit down,' he commanded. 'Let's a have a stiff one.'

Whisky and Coke were wheeled in. So was a fleshy bone.

'Ok, Sam. I've known all along that you working for me wasn't a complete pledge of allegiance. You needed inspiration for a novel, a memoir, whatever. That said, I do believe in your loyalty. On multiple, not zero grounds.'

Here he paused for effect. None forthcoming, he resumed:

'Wanna story? Here goes.'

Gulping a large amount of his drink, his voice grew hazy.

'Been thinking. Came to the conclusion: if I can't be … powerful and, er, er…'

Had he passed out?

No. Suddenly erect like a candle, he declared:

'Being blind didn't work out, right? Became bored with it anyway. So here's the plan: I'll become immortal!'

Sam unbuttoned his blazer with nervous care. D took my lead and the scissors Myriam had left behind. He cut the former with the latter. Freedom can hurt.

'I need your help, team. One last time. One.'

I scratched my ear much as Sam had unbuttoned his blazer.

The idea?

'Sam. Your last name being Carton much influenced my decision to employ you as my speech-writer. Cartoon, by now, would be better. Walt Disney, see, was my hero since I was a kid. Legend had it that he was frozen upon his death to be unfrozen some time or other. I had my people research. More fake news. He was incinerated. But what the hell.'

My friend crossed and uncrossed his legs. A sure sign of exasperation. Unperturbed, D continued.

'Think! What guarantees a legendary status? What muzzles negative publicity forever? When do criminals become martyrs, or phoney artists revered? Think!!'

(Here a dramatic pause.)

'When they die. Death insures immortality! Ironic, ain't it? Ha! What's Jesus' claim to glory and the key of his universal influence? That he got resurrected! Got it?'

We gaped in disbelief. Was D planning to have himself crucified?

'Sam. Find out everything about, whatsitcalled, yeah, well, the technique of freezing bodies. Conic-something. NOW!'

Whereupon he traipsed up the stairs again. Hearing the door slam, I gathered no longer to be needed. Hence I followed Sam to his room.

As usual, he spoke when reading or writing. (I had at some point hoped he did so to mobilise my attention, perhaps even my opinion. That point had blurred. All fixed marks in this house were gradually diluting like a watercolour lashed by rain.)

XII

Cryonics was what D has been alluding to. From the Greek *kryos* meaning cold. Low-temperature, usually at about minus 270 °C (approximately – 460 °F) entails not only the preservation, but possibly the future revival of the body.

So that was what D had in mind! Escape from shame in order to return to fame in some later future!

'Are we surprised?' asked Sam, throwing me a teasing glance.

Instead of sweeping my tail, I slanted my ears. Indicating annoyance.

'Roger,' hushed Sam.

A silly expression, in my canine opinion. Why not Pandora? (It sounds vain, I know. But I am what I am, as the hit song in some musical – aaaaaargh! Forget it. It was called ... *Cats.*)

Anyway.

On he went, his rambling full of exclamation marks. You must be legally dead in order to be cryopreserved. How to pull that stunt? Almost three hundred people in the US had abided by the procedure, with another 1,500 on the waiting list. But D was alive and kicking. Furiously.

Sam sighed then laughed.

'D'you know what the major impediment will be? D, unless really dead, won't be able to freeze his assets. Meaning that Myriam can grab it all. That should *cool* him off!'

Too complicated for me... I just locked my hazel eyes with his, offering solidarity.

'Right you are! I'll call Tony the Doc. Thanks.'

Tony thought out-of-the-box, whatever that contained.

He didn't display the false bonhomie some doctors do; he had, instead, the courage of expressing and displaying asperities, weakness and anger rather than confining himself to lukewarm empathy, as some handshakes suggest – in short, he was the man of the situation. No tedious explanations.

The Doc, as expected, took it in all at once, but not too seriously.

'D'you know that John Huston's uncle, refusing to greet an unpleasant relative, faked a heart attack? Well. He held his breath for so long that he actually died!'

Sip and chuckle.

'If you want to know about Near Death Experiences – read a book called *Seven SIN Songs*, written by a friend of mine. Amusing. Other than that, dear Sam: in surgeries of the aortic arch, hypothermia is used to cool the body while an artificial cardiac arrest is induced in order to minimise the need for oxygen – for half an hour max. This span of time should suffice to have D declared clinically dead. With a little help from a ... corruptible doctor, that is. Plenty around, I take it?'

Another sip.

'As to the trivial matter of money. A vast fortune can be diluted and then solidified into diamond crystals – indistinguishable from crushed ice. Get my drift?'

Sam did.

'Talking about ice. Must put some into the maaaarvelhous Armagnac I was given for my birthday today...'

Oh Lord, thought Sam. The man probably thought I'd call to present greetings. But how to congratulate someone who puts ice into a vintage Armagnac?

As was his wont, D found roundabout ways to skirt laws

and jurisdiction. D like Determination. D like Drama. D like Devil – no: D like Death. Blindness hadn't worked.

He'd then tried accusing former Chairmen Klem of hiring the hit-dwarf. His wife for plotting and faking his signature. Amongst the avalanche of fabricated news, these snowballs had soon melted. Frustrating. But now! To not be or to no longer be, that was the answer. Death meant homage. He already basked in the ensuing attention. In his compartmented quarters, D had the worn-out staff redraw his will. A brilliant idea occurred to him: to leave me, Pandora, a big chunk of his inestimable fortune. There were precedents, like that Helmsley hotel-tycoon woman. Then, of course, he'd follow the Doc's advice. Diamond dust! Clever. Well. His three kids were provided for. In fact, most of his companies had been put in their names long ago. Good move: given a threesome, conflict was inevitable.

Now, the details. All D hated. He was no man inclined to read, let alone subtexts. His lawyers would take care of a post-nup, which would repeal and replace the pre-nup. Paid handsomely, that would be done *in a tick*, as Sam would say.

More urgent matters were on D's mind.

Ultimately, whom could he rely upon?

The Doc. He, for sure, could induce a temporary cardiac arrest and all that shit.

D rushed down the stairs again.

'Sam! Call that Tony nutcase. Now! And call that Duff character, while we're at it. Get on with it!'

XIII

Tony the Doc returned a few days later. Algernon Duff

didn't. Having explored and drilled for oil in Burkina Faso, he had found gold. 'Soon I'll rename my company Duff Water,' he had declared, 'even though sand might become an even bigger issue, even in barren Africa...'

Anyway.

D's one-track mind proceeded on the cryonics track. The more he thought about it, the more attractive it seemed.

A major drawback: hard to control the time and place of his return to life. Brain and tissue had to be protected from damage, he had been told. Only nanotechnology might – *might* being a five-letter word D particularly resented – ensure that his precious, unique cells would be preserved.

The good news? Of the four cryopreservation, or was it vitrification, centres, three were in the US – and one in Russia. (Ha. Putin owed him big time.) In Russia, cryonics fell outside the medical industry. Meaning, outside the law. D liked that. A massive donation to some guy coincidentally named Mr Beast, president of the Molecular Institute of Bioengineering, should take care of the rest.

D was an optimist and the Doc, having watched D through a clinical prism, had stopped drinking in spite of his host pouring down whisky as if there were no tomorrow. No longer a figure of speech.

My Master had had his hair stripe-streaked the colours of the American flag. Sam had managed, only just, to stop stars being tattooed on his waxed chest. Then D would embark on wild ramblings or tirades in staccato mode.

Erratic discourses were by now punctuated by nervous tics. He'd recite articles of the Constitution or rant against Michael Jackson. All of it at the top of his voice – when not gurgling, moaning, or mumbling stubbornly, a smile as flaky as curdled milk floating on his ghostly face.

Sam mused: 'It reminds me of a storm coming up, café chairs being carried in, awnings being rolled up. And then nothing happens – twice.'

'You wait,' Tony replied cryptically.

It all came to a pitch when D declared he was a modern-time pharaoh: he now wanted to be mummified. At once! Whereupon he ordered his most cherished belongings to be shoved into a corner.

The pace and confusion were totally disorienting.

Mrs D having removed her curvaceous self to the Cayman Islands, the walls had been repainted teeth white. I hate white almost as much as my Master hates black.

Thank Wolf for Yvette. She had cooked curried scallops for Tony and Sam and the biggest burgers ever for D and myself.

'Isn't a solemn occasion better than fatal attraction?' D hissed in Sam's direction.

My poor friend shuffled his feet. I lay at D's. Unable to be everywhere, there I remained, droopy-eyed.

D day finally approached.

Something strange was going on, but I couldn't put my muzzle on it.

Tony had enrolled the services of the local doctors, flanked by a brigade of bespectacled assistants.

The engine of a refrigerated van roared outside.

Syringes were laid out on a table, next to various bottles of high-octane alcohol.

D, relishing the commotion, wheezed:

'So?'

Why were Tony and Sam supressing giggles? Why did my Master start singing? I squeezed my head in between trembling paws as D was heaved away.

Of course I managed to tiptoe on all fours under the stretcher, conveniently covered with sheets.

Deadly silence reigned in the huge, dark SUV.

Where, a few dog-minutes later, I heard a peremptory voice.

'New itinerary. To the Cheese Manhattan Bank. It's an executive order!'

The Men in White remained impassive.

Then it hit me. Having overheard Yvette, with her usual suavity, wishing my Master well on his journey to a *maison de repos*. I also remembered Sam and the Doc mumbling something about a cuckoo's rest. I then realised that, far from frozen, both the van and D were overheated.

He frantically tried to wiggle himself out of his toga, terribly tight by any emperor's standards. Or was it a commander-in-chief's uniform? A chef's double-breasted apron? Were metallic straps the latest fashion? Well. Then, he, Capital D, would have it branded and emblazoned in not so distant a future. The van came to a stop. Who was the loony who sung, at a demented pitch of his voice:

> Where ignorance is bliss,
> 'Tis folly to be wise.

Someone smart enough not to be a sage?

I howled.

3

DOUBLE DESIRE

'Why?' snapped the Inspector, rubbing his eyes.
Goddamn allergies. And this was September, no pollen in sight. Psychosomatic? Nope. Even teenage murderers didn't make his blood pressure spike anymore.

Darting ice-blue eyes at him, the thirteen-year-old was the very image of composure. Countless years of facing delinquents told the Inspector that the kid was intelligent – the intriguing brand thereof. A murderer all the same. In his experience, the improbable is always possible.

'It was so easy. That's why.'

No vacillation. No guilt. No fear.

'Easy, hum? What kind of a motive is that?'

'Plenty,' declared Adriana. 'As is boredom. Both too often ignored in crime novels.'

'Pulling my leg?'

'Never pull anyone's. My father suffers from a congenital

limp. Pretty boy, however, a gazelle.'

The Inspector visualised the small corpse drifting like a water lily beneath the cliffs of Dover, their whiteness chiselled against a pastel evening. Its head had been held under till no more bubbles ruffled the surface. And a while ago, the officer at reception had announced a young girl who insisted upon making a confession.

So far, no arrest: she was a minor and there were no formal proofs. Yes, she had told how she had taken the 2:20 train from Sandwich to Martin Mill, a wetsuit and goggles in her bag; walked the two miles to the beach where the kid and his nanny were likely to be found; put on her kit; swam towards the boy, who was always out at sea on his own, as she had noted. She then got on top of him, then dug her thumbs into the arteries of his neck. The practical details in books and on TV. Simple to replicate.

'How did you know you'd find them there?'

'Because that's what the boy and his nanny did every Saturday afternoon until winter set in. Do I really have to reiterate everything I'd been observing?'

The Inspector felt nauseated. Because of the girl? The tuna salad? Might he have grown allergic to fish, and to women, ever younger?

Adriana, arms folded, escaped into hermetic silence. Though there was something fishy about her, she looked pretty much like any other teenager.

As the chances of getting her to tell more dwarfed, he bade her leave through a side door. Her passport, which she had graciously handed over without being prompted to do so, would be kept at the station.

'I made a choice, man,' she snapped, getting up. 'Choices are gambles. Get my drift?'

Whereupon the girl bolted out of the door. Dumbfounded, it took the Inspector a moment to recollect his thoughts.

All he had to go by, for the moment, was a backpack found near the shore and containing the boy's identity documents. The chances of finding reliable witnesses on the train? Improbable. Youngsters had flocked to Dover on that date: a pop concert.

Multi-layered complexity required a club sandwich.

***

'What am I doing here?' Penny hissed at the cop passing, scrutinising the graffitied walls with contempt. 'Unpaid parking tickets can't possibly warrant this formality, can they?'

To soothe her nerves, she scribbled notes regarding the impending redecoration of her dental practice.

The exotic-looking woman facing her was sobbing uncontrollably. In her mid-twenties, she had loser written all over her face, or so Penny thought. She disliked pretty women and losers in equal measure.

Exasperated, she asked her what the matter was. No answer.

'Calm down. My husband should be here shortly. He's good at solving problems.'

'So is mine,' squealed her vis-à-vis, sweeping raven curls aside.

Manda D had come to follow up on the missing-person's case she'd opened two days ago in Dover. Her son's.

Penelope Jones's daughter, though merely thirteen, was prone to disappear for a day or two. Not particularly interested in mischief, for the time being, she'd come back unscathed. Penny put it on the harmless account of the girl seeking attention. A few phone calls usually sufficed to confirm that Adri had slept over at one of her school companions'. Teenagers etc., nowadays. But she'd been gone for three days. As for Neil? Unreachable.

A door swung open. The Inspector, by now scratching the inside of his elbows, told both of them to come in.

He's got amazingly slim fingers, noted Penny. Like a pianist's.

Overweight, thought Manda, but kind, middle-aged face.

A joint convocation was unorthodox. But then, the fact that both kids were surnamed Jones, common or not, had arrested his experienced attention.

It lasted no longer than ten minutes.

The Inspector saw opposite poles. One, pale and bland; the other, Bizet's Carmen type. An untamed shrew? Not quite…Too fragile. Poles have something in common: ice. That's why the expression bipolar shouldn't be synonymous with a manic-depressive: the latter oscillates between flaming fire and simmering embers – not between two extremes of freezing.

But back to facts.

Penelope understood that her adopted daughter was on a rampage.

Manda understood her last remnant of hope to be shattered.

What neither had yet realised, was that their respective children's father was one and the same.

Mrs Jones straightened her unruffled skirt and went ballistic. Barking that she'd get the best lawyer in town, in

England, in the world, she bolted out, much as Adriana had. Mimetics.

After Penelope's stormy departure, Manda had fluttered around like a sleep-flying bat (he'd write the image down on his precious yellow pad).

The Inspector longed to wrap a blanket around her shoulders. Instead, he retrieved allergy eye drops from his pocket. He watched the rain trickling down the window. A downpour about to turn into a deluge. What he saw were tears.

'All right. What next?'

'Would you stop opening all your sentences with "all right"? Nothing was. It's all been wrong.'

He handed Manda another handkerchief.

'Sorry. When did you meet Mr Neil Jones?'

'I need a coffee.'

The inspector buzzed his assistant. 'You were saying?'

'I was born in Morocco. I was raped, beaten, robbed, you name it, at an early age. I managed to escape. To London. Still so young, I learnt to speak proper English. Having been all sorts of things, from supermarket cashier to babysitter, I was employed as a Bunny at the Playboy Club on Park Lane. Fancy. Crazy tips. Drilled to abide by discipline, I endured. Crooks, Earls, Arabs, whatever, enjoyed the pleasure of my company, as they say. I preferred girls. No lesbian but ... yes. I preferred tongues to dicks.'

The Inspector's eyebrows arched.

'Even though I was paid handsomely, I always went back to that dingy flat of mine. By bicycle. Saving for the future, see?'

He did not. No worthwhile future to save for in sight, he'd ever had.

Unexpectedly, she turned from livid to radiant.

'One fine dawn, actually June 21st, the summer solstice, I get hit by a car. It skids on. Another car stops – a man gets out – it was Neil. He brings me home, takes care of my injuries, feeds me, watches over me … and does not rape me. In fact, he starts humming "Strangers in the Night". Out of tune. Made me laugh. He vaguely resembled an actor, can't remember his name…'

'Spare me the girlie talk. Then?'

Manda stood up, brittle as a twig.

'What do you mean by *then*?'

'Get your story straight.'

She grabbed her bag and tiptoed out. Hers was genuine outrage. 'Call me what you like. But remember this: I've always been a devoted mother and faithful to Neil!'

The Inspector's knees itched furiously. This sordid, rather bizarre story strained his nerves.

***

Later that day, Adriana's father – adoptive father – was shown into his office. He should have seen it coming. Two families. Two properties. Two bank accounts. Oh well.

A toothpick into his mouth, the Inspector observed the clearly insecure and exhausted architect. What were his true feelings towards the victim's mother?

'Manda? What's she got to do with this? Something happened to her?'

'She left a short while ago. Please answer, sir.'

The two men took each other's measure whilst appreciating the distance. At first sight, nothing in common. Yet both sensed an undercurrent that just might connect them.

Shrugging, much weight on his shoulders an impediment, Neil Jones murmured:

'It started as a casual affair.'

No conniving glance. Adulterous husbands had a knack for throwing them.

'But then, something unusual happened. I discovered happiness.'

Not a word often heard on these premises.

'Meaning?'

'What I said. After about fourteen years married to a woman cool as marble and smooth as an eel, I came across volcanic Manda ... fire played with me.'

The man sighs. A sincere sigh.

'Was I longing to burn? Possibly. One does consent to fall into a trap of one's own making.'

Not immune to what some call the Scotland Yard syndrome, and all the more exposed to it for being a playwright at heart, the Inspector reminded himself to skirt empathy.

No question forthcoming, Neil Jones figured some graphics were called for.

'As I said: routine at home. Security and safety in one hand. Danger and drama on the other. Complementary contrasts. Point being that my life drastically and dramatically changed after what people call the *other* woman became pregnant...'

'You don't seem the type,' the Inspector mumbled.

'Don't trust the obvious.'

The architect, a Mel Gibson semi-clone, threw his hands heavenwards.

'I did not act on whim. I reacted to double desire. No dilemma.'

Though, when at work, the Inspector's imagination was

seldom ignited, it now flared up. Duality! He knew a thing or two about that. But better keep focused.

'Alliterations a professional deviance?'

'Call it symmetry.'

'Not in the mood for semantic subtleties.'

The spoof was lost on the architect.

'Just describe your personal circumstances, sir, and make it simple.'

Neil Jones hesitated, then proceeded to embark upon a long monologue. So long, in fact, it seemed a release from an overload of solitude.

'All right, sir. That'll be it for now. We'll reconvene tomorrow.'

Jones's demeanour, unlike that of most wealthy people, suggested resignation. 'Please leave through the side door, as did your daughter.'

'My daughter?' Jones exclaimed, utterly bewildered. 'Isn't this about tax evasion, fraud or whatever it's called?'

Good Lord. The guy really hadn't got a clue. He had been picked up at Heathrow some hours earlier, disembarking from a Swissair flight from Lugano. In these pre-cellular phones, pre-internet times, it had been impossible to locate him earlier.

***

Time for a botched report. The Inspector was a fast writer.

His superior, the Detective Chief Superintendent, read it diagonally and declared the matter of no special interest. 'Wrap it up asap. Must go.'!

His more personal version:

Adriana's adoptive parents, Mr and Mrs Jones, had been

college sweethearts. Furiously besotted, Penelope had pretended to be pregnant in order to get handsome and elusive Neil to propose marriage.

Not only did she lie; it turned out, later on, that she was sterile – for reasons irrelevant here.

Though reluctantly, her parents financed his studies. That their son-in-law had set his mind on so hazardous a future as architecture – bad luck. Their daughter, for one, would follow traditional footsteps: dentists for three generations. They had something else to gloat about, for the resemblance between Diana Spencer, the future Queen, and Penny was startling.

To marry a man called Jones of all surnames ... most unfortunate. A bit of a cripple, on top. Yet. Having climbed the Triple A ladder (Ascot, Asprey, Annabel's) what could they do other than stiffening the upper lip?

By 1988, when Penny and Neil celebrated their seventh wedding anniversary, the architect had become an international star in his domain: the construction of museums. They moved to Belgravia Square. Their parties were the toast of the town and Penelope, as she now insisted on being called, became known for her taste – Renaissance furniture, Persian hand-knotted carpets, Murano candelabras and other ostentatious valuables all over the place.

Was the marriage already on the rocks or still on the ropes?

'Do you know the feeling of hanging on to a situation, call it a marriage, the way you don't close a book because you're halfway through, even though it's bad?' Jones had shrugged.

That very night, Penelope presented him with a fait accompli: the adoption of a baby girl. Displaying a chubby piece of meat (again, Jones's words) clad in a pink-stripped sailor suit, she announced that it was to be called Adriana.

'Having always feared that any departure from comfort would stymy creativity, this one boosted it. I started working harder than ever and whenever possible, abroad.'

Then he meets Manda D. Passion vs. perfection. So far, so good: another boost of vitality. But a child is born. The victim.

The Inspector had lost his trust in wishful thinking. Yet he suddenly wished the young women had lingered on.

The door creaked. Manda had forgotten her umbrella. She timidly apologised for her former brusqueness.

'Fancy a drink?' he heard himself asking.

'You're insane,' she riposted without indignation. 'Do you realise my son lies dead? Murdered.'

'I do. Let's go.' He took her to his local pub. She'd find its hum and hub soothing – or so he fathomed.

They played darts. She never hit the target but laughed. Feeling guilty to be able to, letting it happen was soothing.

'You must eat something.'

'Not hungry.'

The Inspector ordered all the same. She devoured the food.

'Have you always fended for yourself?' he gently asked. 'No relatives? No best friend? No…?'

'Only Neil.'

The architect's profile invaded his visual field. The man's eyes emanated kindness, yes, but also indecision. A self-made man, but somewhat spineless. His wife, Penelope, was the boss. Not only one-track minded but 'cool and slick as an eel', or something like that, as Neil Jones had put it.

The Inspector emerged from his rêverie. Manda having stepped out to catch some fresh air, he swiftly dotted down some notes on his pad. Recapitulating:

a) The architect becomes prominent. Commutes in jets, often private. At home, he must perform again: the success story and caring-husband role. Among many other nuisances, Adriana bears an uncanny resemblance to her adoptive mother. Coincidence.

b) Adriana was the killer. She confessed. Someone, he had been informed earlier on, had mentioned an androgynous blonde wearing a wetsuit and flippers. The description, time and all, fitted.

But c) and most importantly: why kill the young boy? Why not his mother? Had Adriana discovered Neil's double life, the Moroccan would have been a more logical target.

Perched on the pub stool again, the young woman looked forlorn. Experience prompted the Inspector to ask whether he could call her by her first name. It often triggered comfort.

'Yes.'

He liked that about Manda. No rodeos.

Suddenly she burst into tears again. Vestigial pain compounding all else?

Just as suddenly, he felt enraged. That Penelope woman had shown no emotion whatsoever. Might she be the guiltiest of the lot?

The Inspector hailed a cab to bring Manda home. She remained silent as – a tomb. (Too much of a cliché for pen to be put to paper.)

***

Seated at his kitchen table, Tchaikovsky's violin concerto on high volume, he felt bitter.

Why had he not been able to impose his wishes or to assert his talent? He'd had nothing but A grades in his drama and literature courses. Why had he let his dominating mother, harping on the chords of duty and on the spectre of his father's weakness, coax him into an existence devoted to order, if not law?

Alcohol exacerbated his regrets; music enhanced concentration.

Melancholy, another side effect of booze, kicked in.

Were most adults coerced into caricatures from an early age? What about the thirteen-year-old, an orphan from Bulgaria? Had Adriana, whilst being taught impeccable manners and speech, been conditioned to unscrupulous action? Reproducing a pattern Penelope might have been straitjacketed into herself?

Mothers.

He retrieved the yellow pad from his jacket. Only the written word could sweep away his spleen.

PENELOPE'S MOTHER (mellow): Don't you think you have over-indulged Adri?

PENNY (irritated): Last time I checked, you reproached me being self-absorbed and egocentric.

MOTHER: No contradiction. (Sighs.) Your father much the same, may he rest in hell.

PENNY (jumps): Mum? How dare you?

MOTHER: Merely emulating your crudeness. Like it or not, you are my flesh and blood. We, at least, didn't need an agency's stamp to attest an acceptable provenance...

PENNY: ...my father's parenthood? Do you only recall how many affairs you had or when?

MOTHER (icy like a Hitchcock icon): Have you ever wondered why Adriana developed such blatant hostility towards Neil?

PENNY: You exaggerate.

MOTHER: Do I really? First you impose a child. Then you become overbearing. Transform it, or her, into your creature. Age three, she is dressed like you, Baby Dior and all. Then the ballet classes you wish you hadn't dropped out of. And then, of course, the books…

PENNY: … encouraging her to read? Is that objectionable?

MOTHER: Not at all – had you not persuaded her fairy tales to be a waste of hope, poems a waste of dreams, and romance, in whichever form, fraudulent.

PENNY (aghast): Look now, lady. The girl was born in the slums of Bucharest. Violence was her natural environment. Her fascination for crime novels, detective stories, whatever, wasn't my doing. And yes, I encouraged it – I like inquisitive minds.

MOTHER: …precociously so.

PENNY (though fidgety, folds her napkin into a neat triangle): So what?

MOTHER (throwing hers on the table): Are you faithful to Neil?

PENNY (outraged): Of course I am!

MOTHER: Why?

PENNY: …

MOTHER: Are you in love?

PENNY: Who? Me? Him?

The Inspector opens another beer. This is getting tedious. Yet a scene must come to a conclusion, must it not? Forget the love bit. He'd erase it. Where was he? Yes. Faithfulness.

MOTHER: Good. It simplifies life.

PENNY (smiling for the first time): It does. Besides, there's little chance of flirting as a dentist. Open mouths with metal clips, see?

MOTHER (smirks): Pen, sometimes I wish you had weaknesses. Really I do. Booze, if not men. Drugs. Stealing cars. Don't know ... some deviance from convention, see?

PENNY (cringing): Drop it.

MOTHER: So I shall. You're never tempted, that's the problem. All iron, no velvet. In that, we differ. But I, for one, wasn't a control freak. (Her eyes cloud.) What for? You were born self-controlled. No tears, no tantrums. Perhaps because during the first three years of your life, the crucial ones as they say – whoever *they* are – you were left to your own devices... Nanny can't-remember-her-name's too busy emulating Julie Driscoll, Mary Quant, whatever silly role models there were in the sixties...

PENNY: Yeah.

MOTHER (stern): In my presence, it's YES, not yeah.

PENNY: F.O.

MOTHER (with a grimace): I protected you against the anguish of solitude. Sport helped, of course. Made you competitive, kept you busy, created a sense of...

PENNY (tense again): Sure. It sure distracted me from realising, early on, the extent of your duplicity. Father knowing, but looking the other way – mostly at the nannies he didn't exactly select for their competence, or so you claim – or else at me. Expecting too much. (She sweeps away breadcrumbs off the tablecloth and imaginary dust off her blazer.) Must go to the ladies' room.

Heaving with relief, MOTHER hails the waiter, slips him a lavish tip and orders another Irish coffee to be served in a tea mug. He winks.

PENNY (back): Oh? You paid?
MOTHER: I did.
PENNY: Thought invitations were meant to be enjoyable.
MOTHER: Ever so kind.

The Inspector threw his scribbled sheets in the nearby bin.
  Compliance. Control. Contradictions. Crucial. (Had
the architect's lingo contaminated him?)
  Time for TV and food.

***

The following day, he was handed several folders.
  Scotland Yard's investigation skills and international
connections could be relied upon.
  (And his mind, to ornate the gaps...)
  He tossed Penelope Jones's file away. What you see is
what there is, he scoffed. A rather monolithic personal-
ity. Of the 'Ladies-Who-Have-Lunch' and 'A Person From
Somewhere' kind. Clever but not intelligent.
  Manda's profile, as he suspected, was far more ambiguous.
  She had been named thus by a Father who revered
Mandela. A Rhodesian-born former Foreign Legion mercenary, he had, after many turns and twists, ended up as
a bodyguard to the highest bidder. His Moroccan wife
had left him when the kid was only three years old. For a
dentist! The improbable always possible, etc.
  So here is Manda, shuttled from one Middle-Eastern
country to another. Her father is a bully. Having hoped
to produce a son and a soldier, he inculcates masculine
behaviour.
  Age seventeen, she packs nothing much to go nowhere

particular. She just leaves. Casablanca's streets are deserted. A middle-aged man wearing a gold watch finds her shivering in an embryo position under a porch in shambles. He takes her to his flat. There is a fireplace. He first feeds, then rapes her. She feels neither pain nor pleasure. He buys her dresses and a new identity – meaning a passport. She learns to please the man in exchange for protection. Does Manda realise that she is performing what, clinically speaking, is sex? First and foremost she perceives it as a currency and a token. How harrowing an experience was that?

The Inspector sharpened his pencil.

A crime had been committed. An innocent life snapped. Strangled, drowned – actually both. Deed done by a thirteen-year-old kid displaying not a scintilla of remorse. Her 'mother', a woman too immersed in her myopic cocoon to embrace the emotional panorama written all over the wall. Manda, an emotionally orphaned woman who, though having roamed the streets, wasn't what one calls streetwise. No: too trusting for that.

At the nexus, the architect.

Neil J. is married and successful. Satisfied? Angry? Not mutually exclusive. His wife's unilateral decision to introduce an alien – Adriana – into their predictable life creates a disturbance he hasn't bargained, let alone been prepared, for. He no longer feels at home in his own house: nannies, screaming, and other disturbances shatter a lukewarm peace made of unspoken compromises. Yet, as he had said, it gave his life a jolt.

One tender night, Jones witnesses a pretty girl hit by a car. He takes care of her. She embodies everything Neil has never known: vulnerability, sulphuric looks, ambiguous eroticism. For once, he feels useful. His desire to protect overwhelms him. In fact, he is grateful to her for making him feel needed. A parallel life – the alternative to a parade life – opens up like a double-glazed window (or is it a masked one-way mirror?).s

Tossing his pad aside, the Inspector decided to summon the architect to his office, first thing after noon. He took a shower and sank into an oneiric sleep.

***

The man never showed up.

Adriana remained under house arrest.

Manda would not answer his calls.

He ignored Penelope's lawyer's calls.

Four days had now elapsed since the corpse of the seven-year-old had been found floating in St Margaret's Bay. The image of the small bluish, wrinkled, dissolving body kept invading his retina.

It was late again and the Inspector, tipsy from insomnia, hummed Arnold-whatever-his-name's poem. 'Dover Beach'.

> The sea is calm tonight.
> The tide is full, the moon lies fair
> Upon the straits;...
> Listen! You hear the grating roar
> Of pebbles which the waves drew back, and fling,
> At their return, up the high strand,
> Begin, and cease, and then again begin
> With tremulous cadence slow, and bring
> The eternal note of sadness in.

A romantic, he felt lulled by the melody. Not for long.

At five in the morning, the Inspector roamed his flat, sweating profusely. For there was the usual glitch in drowning cases: no fingerprints, neither on the victim nor on the perpetuator. One hand washes the other, as the biblical (was it?) saying goes. Replace the other's hand by the other's neck, and...

His job was to hammer in evidence. Other than the boy's death and his half-sister's confession, not much to go on. Besides: did he really want to dig further? Hadn't enough existences been shattered by vindication to wreck their remains?

His thoughts started slaloming. Writing always helped.

What had Neil, Penny and Manda in common, other than being only children? Usually meaning introspective self-sufficiency?

And why could he not help but sympathise with that Jones fellow? Unwilling to elaborate on his own past, the Inspector's brain stalled. All things considered, the protagonists involved were of no magnetic interest. Were compulsive lies a common denominator? If so, so what?

Only the other night he had listened to an interview with a psychologist from UCAL. 'We lie at least four times in the first ten minutes of interaction with someone. It's part of the social contract.'

The Inspector had experienced it at first-hand, many times over. Yet the fellow's concluding formula stuck: 'We lie in order not to kill one another.'

Granted: it requires a lot of ruse to lead a double life; to yield to double desires and, so far as Adriana was concerned, to plan, commit, then confess murder – all the while looking neither like an innocent lamb, nor pretending to be.

Might this particular case represent an opportunity to emulate Truman Capote's 'faction' *In Cold Blood* based on a rather banal *fait divers*? Could investigation, coupled with a twisted narrative, lead to notoriety? Take Somerset Maugham, a former doctor...

Imperative: avoid sequitur mania.

(Sigh.)

Meanwhile, Neil was tossing in bed. His conscience dictated one and only way to behave: face the requiem. Tell Penny; then leave her.

Cruel as it sounded, what would he not give for things to be the other way round? Adrian, his own child, still alive; spooky Adriana at the bottom of some freaking ocean...

How had he tumbled into such a mess?

He had loved, yes, loved, both his wife and his mistress. In totally different ways. Gratitude was the foundation of his marriage; wasn't it also gratitude, albeit of a diametrically different kind, which melded him to Manda?

Was he – had he – fucked up?

Had he been fooled? First and foremost by himself?

Pulpous, provocative, promiscuous Manda had initially been repelled by sex. Precisely that, nutty as it may sound, had turned him on. Not only mentally. Her imperviousness to pleasure had ignited unknown sensations. Extramarital affairs, to him, had until then been recreational. Quick interludes followed by a stiff drink and, more often than not, a swift financial transaction. 'Dipping done,' he'd grin, grateful to put the stigma of his limp behind him for a while.

When he told the above to the Inspector, the latter chewed on his pencil, pondering the colloquial expression 'to get lucky'. Did Seneca, who'd defined luck as a situation 'when preparation meets opportunity,' have sexual intercourse in mind. Ha.

Manda's frigidity had, Neil had continued, been a shield, a protection against the repeated intrusions into her body she had consented to for the sake of survival. Her violent father had inculcated the power of resilience. In England, she'd been drawn into dubious dregs. And yet, miraculously, Manda had remained a virgin at the core; in her very own way, intact.

'How did you manage to keep your double life secret? That wife of yours, Penelope, doesn't strike me as stupid. You had been married for seven years when she adopted the three-year-old girl. You meet Manda two years later, right?'

'Correct.'

'Your son was born on May 2nd 1990. Right?'

'Correct.'

'We are now September 28th, 1997. You just turned thirty-nine.'

Loosening his tie, the architect examined the Inspector. Likeable. Weary with his personae. That made two of them. Yet the guy didn't look like someone prone to clashing impulses. Could he emotionally understand how one feels after a beloved son has been eliminated by an unloved daughter? Did the Inspector have kids?

'Nope,' was the laconic response. 'Leading to the overdue question: how did yours, I mean kids, meet?'

Neil reached into his pocket and retrieved a pill.

'No idea. May I have some water please?'

'With a shot of whisky?'

'Nice, Inspector.'

'Huh. Are you going to swallow a Valium or something along those lines?'

'Correct.'

The Inspector jumped to his feet – well, not quite, given his weight. Having retrieved a bottle from his cupboard, he sunk into his chair again, and let it swirl towards the window. He folded his hands over his belly; his habit when releasing tension.

'My interest in this matter isn't altogether noble. I must admit that your story – your ordeal – intrigues me beyond a strictly professional framework.'

'So I gathered. You strike me as a … writer, if you don't mind me venturing.'

In spite of the radiators, both men shivered.

'Shall we have dinner? It's too gloomy in here.'

The Inspector hesitated. Unethical, perhaps, but so what? Truth be told, he was fed up with tinned beans at home or lousy pub food.

'Would the Savoy suit you?'

***

The maître d' greeted Neil Jones effusively.

'The corner table as usual, sir?'

Led across the wood-panelled room, the Inspector grumbled, 'Your canteen?'

'Only on Saturday nights – when not in Kent, that is. Penny hates the place, calls it stiff and stuffy.'

The best sirloin steak ever (he had almost ordered a Dover sole, but then – yes.) A Château Lafitte. Fresh-baked bread. Irish butter. The flicker of a fireplace.

Most enticing was the architect's company. The man was

gentle. Moreover, not one to beat around the bush.

'A double life requires circumspection and concentration. Have I said that before? Never mind: it's of the essence. Annie, my secretary, helped. Call her an accomplice. Poor lady, raised a Catholic, but strict about nothing, especially not Cuba Libres. Anyway. Opposite my desk, two boards pinned with post-its, reminding me of birthdays, presents, bank transfers, schedules, plus what I had said or promised to each – Penny and Manda, Adriana and – Adrian.'

The Inspector scratched his neck.

'I know. But my wife had had everything embroidered or engraved with the initials AJ upon adopting the girl. I just thought … should I die, it would be, you know … practical. I'd have preferred Hadrian, like the Roman Emperor, but…'

'I presume you bought both women the same perfume.'

The architect grinned. Had he momentarily forgotten his son had been drowned? Was he harpooned by despair himself or had the effect of the tranquilisers, compounded by the booze, merely mellowed him? Suits me fine, thought the Inspector. In Valium veritas and all that.

'Quite. You have a foxy mind, if I might say so.'

Neil snapped out of his haze.

'Inspector, I've always been fond of children. Genuinely. D'you know why I decided to become an architect?'

'Should I?'

'Voilà. At ten years old or so, I started designing mini-golf courses. Damn difficult. The velocity of curves and turns, of tunnels, calculating gravity, you get the idea. Then – a long story I'll spare the both of us. Finally, kid-friendly museums. My claim to fame, as you probably know. Museums used to be shunned by the young, who found them boring. My projects integrate toboggans, cartoons, special effects, etc. To associate art with fun instead of tedium. Follow me?'

The Inspector did. Neil Jones was a liar, but no fraud.

Both men started to yawn – then stopped abruptly.

Statuesque, clad in an embroidered black long dress, the Moroccan stood in front of them.

'Princess!' exclaimed the architect. 'How...'

'Did I know where to find you? Oh Archi!'

Her voice was reproachful, yet devoid of animosity.

'But...'

'I've been waiting and waiting more. You didn't...'

'Princess! I sent two letters and daily bouquets of mauve dahlias! The flowers for apology, gratitude, the token of...'

'It's your arms I need, Archi, your arms around me!'

Visibly robbed of strength, she slumped at Neil's feet, an image of bereavement and frailty.

The Inspector, not too steady on his legs himself, heaved himself to the door of the restaurant. Bloody bastard! Hadn't even gone to visit his dead son's mother since the tragedy!

On the threshold, he turned around. The architect had slouched to the floor and, kneeling next to Manda, cradled her as one does a baby. The maître d' looked the other way. Manners.

***

Looking demure, the teenager observed the Inspector's glass sizzling with Alka-Seltzer with a wolfish eye.

Penelope had dropped Adriana at the police station, asking to be called when the interrogation, interview, whatever they called it, what the heck, was over. Bye.

Bitch, thought the Inspector. What a so-called family!

Another bloody Sunday. Though not feeling up to it, this tricky exchange was a must, the first hearing in court scheduled for tomorrow.

'Young lady, I'm tired. Hope you realise how privileged you were not to be locked up since ... the event.'

'Don't care. No problem.'

'Drowning a half-brother not a problem either?'

'It's done.'

The Inspector infused a camomile teabag into lukewarm water. Disgusting. He retrieved the malt from his cupboard.

'Want some?'

'I don't drink, sir. I'm thirteen, remember?'

'Ah! Too young to drink, but not to kill?'

'Your words.'

She smiled. Most reluctantly, he found her smile disarming. The girl obviously realised the gravity of her deed but didn't perceive it as an injustice. She displayed something he had seldom come across: intense indifference.

Disconcerting, that's what she was. Not that the Inspector's convictions were assailed; he had never harboured a whole lot of them. But confusion was something unfamiliar.

'When did you cross the line from virtual to actual deed?' he sighed.

'Long story.'

'Do tell.'

'Sure?'

'I must write a report, remember?'

'Poor guy,' Adriana un-coquettishly wiggled.

The Inspector rolled a carbon-paper into his antique

Remington. He was a man of tradition.

'Okay. I've read detective and crime stories from an early age on. My dream? To become a PI – no nurse, no Claudia Schiffer, no astronaut, not even a stewardess, least of all some sort of virtuous housewife. I'm spellbound by excesses. Transgressions. Weirdness. See?'

'Should I?'

Adriana waved the question aside as one does a fly.

'Neither ambition nor monotony in my chords. Nor in yours, man...or so what I'm driven by, call it instinct, tells me.'

Was the tone heinous – or simply honed?

'Adriana. Tomorrow, your future's at stake. Answer or don't. You did it because it was easy – or so you said. But that innocent seven-year-old puppy, honestly...?'

The girl's tone changed from arrogant to whiny.

'He robbed me of the love I deserved. He usurped my uniqueness. Hey. That namesake impostor was about to smash any semblance of a family that...'

The Inspector wasn't moved.

'When and where did you discover Adrian existed?'

Back to her initial attitude, she snapped:

'Are you dim or what? My mother inherited a house in Sandwich. The place, not the food, man. My father bought a place on St Margaret's Bay. Have a map? Thought so. Approximately ten miles or so away from one another. White Cliffs of Dover, get it? Where Noël Coward and Ian Fleming, should the names ring a bell or two, had properties.'

The Inspector scratched his left wrist.

'Gradually, last summer in fact, I suspected my so-called father was cheating on my so-called mother. Penelope indeed. Know what the name comes from? Oh Jeez. *Encyclopaedia Britannica*, ever heard of it?'

He could see why Neil Jones would be put off by her haughtiness, added to the tattoos and messy hair. All of it provocation. He began suspecting the thirteen-year-old to be a born, masterful and very articulate manipulator. But then again … the girl exuded some sort of perverse naivety.

'Does it all boil down to jealousy?'

'Not so simple.'

She tossed a bulky envelope on his desk.

'Wrap your eyes around this. Supposing you can read.'

He swept the envelope aside.

'You're about to arrested, young girl. Offence to a…'

'Always have been. Fuck you too.'

The Inspector stood up, kicking his chair out of the way.

'Wish I could feel sorry for you. But I don't pity monsters.'

'Nor I queens,' giggled Adriana. 'No drags needed!'

Touché. And it hurt. Even his colleagues suspected him to be a fag. Mistakenly. Asexual, that's what he was. About to say so, he recoiled: what explanations did he owe the brat? She'd probably come out with some psychobabble retrieved from her books.

'Inspector. Mine is no crime of passion. There are no mitigating, exonerating and all that jazz circumstances. I was driven by a combination of the three impulses that underlie most criminal behaviour.'

She threw him a furtive glance.

'Here goes: most murderers have suffered from some traumatic affective loss – in my case, being abandoned no sooner born; a symbolic loss – in my case, discovering I was no longer a sole child, adopted or not; finally, material loss – not my case, my mother being wealthy in her own right. Besides, I'm smart enough to sort life out on my own.'

'After being released from jail or some such, if ever,' he riposted.

'I'm well aware of what's awaiting me. Rather looking forward to it. Interesting experience, if you ask me. Might we return to the point? My motive? My psychological profile? Huh? Well. It all boils down to neurotic narcissism.'

The Inspector could not help but show bafflement.

'Look it up, man. See you in court, as they say. Now please call my mother. If you can remember how to dial, that is.'

***

First letter in the envelope.

'My lover my saviour.
Fifteen months and three days since we met.

Five months since I discovered I was pregnant – that date coincided with my discovery of how joyful sex could be. Ironic it's assumed that pregnancy doesn't know the word, bad for desire?

Oh my darling! To think the miracle happened on a first of April! Too foolish to be true I remember it so well.

As you know, Archi, I was what is called frigid. Slowly, very slowly, you diluted my torments. After a while, I no longer feel assaulted when penetrated. Yet you caused a new pain I became hooked. Domination, not a torture now a need. No sooner you gone I crave for your penis in my pussy and our mixed juices.

I miss being gently whipped the savage of our delicious

deliriums repulsion and rapture. Cuffs. Muzzles. Blindfolds. Oh darling! No limit to perversity when tender! Docility makes me dizzy I want to lick, suck, bite, squeeze you into galvanising, you said the word, pleasure. I want YOU. My body to twist and turn at will and whim. We must explore and transgress more.

My love: fuck take and keep me. Allow surrender as mine.

About fucking ... would you tell your wife to f-off, as you have been promising for ... seven years, a number as magic as is my faith? —M.

Two more letters sprinkled with words like 'convolution', 'palpitation', 'velvety tongue', 'clitoris', 'cock', subdued the Inspector's short-lived erection. Scratching his thighs was a side effect of allergy, not of arousal.

He imagined Adriana, aged twelve or so, reading these lines. A tough cookie, she'd probably be more deeply shaken by the betrayal than by the vocabulary. (Pernicious TV and all that.)

Neil's pledge to leave what Adriana clung on to as a symbol of legitimacy upset her most. Learning that a parallel family existed, her adoptive father and his mistress having had a son exacerbated the pain – the fear? Sheer vexation? Might she have overheard her mother lamenting not having been able to engender one?

If so, all would have made sense: Neil's disregard for her – or was it plain rejection? His absent-mindedness. His almost permanent absence.

The Inspector's speculations were based on what the girl had elaborated on earlier, whilst waiting for her mother to pick her up – Penelope Jones in no hurry, it had seemed.

'What would my heroes, Sherlock Holmes, Hercule

Poirot, Miss Marple, even Colombo have done? Exactly.'

Adriana's voice had turned into a whisper.

'So I follow my father – yeah, know who I mean. Am taken aback by the maelstrom reigning in Soho; by the smoky restaurant into which Neil saunters to embrace a rather fat but yes, beautiful woman, with a feverish expression. I'd never seen emotion flicker on his face before. Let alone such contrast in setting: Soho? Planets away from Belgravia's galaxy.'

The girl paused, as if seeking compassion or disapproval. What she encountered was a rather sarcastic look. Yes, she realised: the way I talk isn't typical of a teenager. I sound like one of the many books I read. But – that's the way I am and it is. I'm not what they call *normal*. To hell with it.

'My nose against the window, I wait. It isn't very long before a nanny, judging from her clothes, walks in, holding a young boy's hand. Neil and the woman's child, obviously.'

That ambivalent look again.

'Having taken the classical precaution of wearing a wig and anodyne clothes, I sit at the closest table without eliciting so much as sideway look. This is how I discover the young boy is called Adrian.'

(Here, the girl's account becomes muddled: the girl cannot uphold her aloofness.)

From what the Inspector pieced together:

Such is the collision of emotions that she rushes out to throw up. It's too unfair!

Does her resolve to remove the (not) bastard from the map crystallise there and then? In a smoky restaurant, perchance?

If so, she hadn't figured out how, for she didn't know, yet, that Neil would, unwillingly, add opportunity to motive.

This she would learn a week later.

Same place, same scenario. 'My adorable Princess,' (here Neil kisses Manda's bronzed hand) 'I've bought a small house above St Margaret's Bay. That way we'll be able to be reunited even on weekends. I'll pretend to play golf or something. She'll never check, too busy with herself...'

She? Penny or herself, wondered Adriana?

'We'll send the boy to the beach with Nanny. He so loves the sea,' Neil murmured, conspiratorially. 'Allowing us to savour the most forbidden...'

Indignation now coalesced with an urge for vengeance. Her 'father' was guilty on the counts of betrayal, of cheating, of leading a double life – in short, of lying in a big huge way.

Was it then that images of drowning surfaced? So to speak?

***

The Inspector shrugged. You can demonise alcohol. But it's hard to deny that it connects dots.

Time for the yellow pad and another pint.

What had happened at the Savoy Oak Room after he left? Why did Manda call Neil 'Archi'? Presumably an abbreviation of architect.

MANDA (shaking): Why, Archi, why?

NEIL (stuttering): Adriana has always been ... cruel, unpredictable, hostile. Whether her infancy in some Bulgarian slum or other explains it or not, she's ... heartless.

MANDA: As is your wife?

NEIL (recoiling): Let's leave her out of this, please.

They both get up, then sit down again, much to the maître d's relief. Though invisible, in the Jeeves tradition, he has followed developments at first hand (hush-hush dinners, often followed by room service) with sober interest. A month or so ago, there had been a twist in the tale. Mrs Jones – the real one – popping in, taking him aside, a bulky envelope meant to bribe him into indiscretion.

'Penelope Jones,' she had declared. 'Am I right in supposing my husband has his … habits with another woman, right here, on Saturday nights?'

The maître d' was a well-read man, especially with regard to mythology: Penelope had been praised for her fidelity to her husband, Ulysses, during the twenty years during which the warrior fought in the Trojan wars or against the Cyclops. One version. The other depicted her as a cunning weaver who had slept with all her 108 suitors whilst displaying, in public, crossed legs and rosy cheeks. She had not welcomed her husband home.

Instinctively, the maître d' remained evasive. Besides, he liked the architect and, by Jove, the taciturn girl too.

Mrs Jones left frustrated. The maître d' had been surprised to see a rather small girl waiting outside.

Verbatim what he would tell the Inspector, under the seal of confidentiality.

Where was he? Yes:

MANDA (jerky again): How could you not come to me? For days and nights on end? Have you been crying? Did they lock you up? Have you slept at all?
NEIL (gulping down a third brandy): I'm under police scrutiny. Perhaps followed. Adriana's…
MANDA (her fists so tense they had become rigid): Never

mention name again! Never ever!

Silence lingers.

MANDA asks for a whisky sour. A Muslim, it's the first time she drinks alcohol, the maître d' registers.

NEIL (shocked): Princess, what are you doing?

MANDA: Same as you.

More silence, increasingly leaden.

MANDA: And now?

NEIL: Sorry?

MANDA (head askew, tears welling): I'm alone again. More than ever. We can have another child, you know? Help me. I beg you!

NEIL (glassy-eyed): How can you think of the future in a situation like this?

MANDA: Hope's a buoy. Archi. I need it.

NEIL (hoping to spot the maître d', in vain): Princess. We must drift under the bridge before crossing it. Court cases can stretch forever. Let it be. Until then.

MANDA: Let *what* be? Your legitimate wife and your adopted daughter? The very one who killed our sweet Adrian?

Her mascara is smudged. Her shoulders sag. She looks not a bit like the sexy creature Neil was irresistibly drawn to. If only he could disentangle himself from this situation…

Suddenly he longs for the safe harbour of his predictable home, for his study where he can draw in peace; for silence.

Silence!

MANDA (pleading): Please let's return to our Soho love nest. Pleeease. Archi! If you don't, I die too.'

Meaning? That she'd kill herself? NEIL can't help... Cursing himself, he limps away.

***

The inspector hailed a cab.

She opened the door without even asking who rung.

Wearing a green kaftan matching her eyes, Manda looked lovely. As did her small flat: shades of ochre, scented candles, deep sofas and kilims.

But – no trace of a child. No toy. No photograph. Manda was a Muslim, but still. The Inspector longed to see the bedrooms but decency forbade asking. A search warrant? On what grounds? Personal curiosity wasn't one of them.

'What do you want?' she enquired, eyebrows raised.

'Just checking you're … safe. Sorry.'

An awkward pause later:

'Come in, will you? You look like someone in need of a mint-tea.'

No connoisseur of the occidental psyche.

'Teasing. A whisky?'

'Sounds better.'

'Famous Grouse. Neil's favourite. What brings you here? Truthfully?'

Letting the ice cubes clink against his glass and watching her bare feet, he too wondered. What indeed?

'Don't exactly know.'

'I saw you at the Savoy, sir. Or better said, I saw you leaving.'

The Inspector crossed his hands over his belly.

'So you did.'

'The whole thing was an act performed for your benefit.'

He goggled then gulped. She sighed.

'Yes. We knew you'd watch.'

'But…'

'Teasing again, sir. Better than crying, you know?'

All right. If she wanted to play, he was game.

'Manda, I had a bug placed under the table. Just in case. No offence meant.'

'None taken.'

Were he ever to transform this story into a play, its title would be: *Abuse*. All the protagonists, the whole lot of them, displayed it one way or another to varying degrees. Or so his experience suggested.

'Manda, where did you learn such good English?'

'Watching porno movies, where else?'

He gazed out of the window.

'You're good at mental ping-pong, Manda.'

'An acquired knack, Inspector. Shared with many who have been conditioned to always swim upstream.'

No sooner uttered, the words made her cringe.

Tempted, for a split second, to riposte 'underwater?', the Inspector shut up. He missed his swirling chair.

'May I be, er, indiscreet?'

'Mustn't you?'

'All right – sorry. I mean, yes. Did you ask Neil how his, er, wife was reacting?'

'I also asked him, for the first time ever, whether he still slept with her.'

As the young woman refilled her ridiculous mug emblazoned with the edelweiss, he weighed the appropriateness of his next question.

'Manda. Where were you on that Saturday afternoon? And where on earth is Adrian's nanny? According to Adriana, she'd fallen asleep, the sun having made her dizzy. Mid-September in Kent? Just before sunset? Please! Since then, no trace of her.'

Manda's gaze clouded.

'My fault. I became so aggressive … afterwards, that she scampered – do you say that?'

'She'll have to testify in court, as I'm sure you know.'

The Moroccan fiddled with her black curls.

'No idea where to look for. Neil paid her cash. No social security number and no valid papers either. As you, sir, will have noticed.'

He didn't. The elderly woman had, in the list of priorities, slipped from under Scotland Yard's radar. Shit.

'She suffered from diabetes. But she also had a sweet tooth and might have been overdosing on chocolate or something…'

The young woman was doing her best to retain her composure. Admirable. But again, Manda's mix of humility and caprice inspired protectiveness.

'Please leave. I'm dead. Oh no! Did I say that?'

She belatedly answered the Inspector's prior question.

'Neil says that his wife rejects him and everything he stands for. That now she wants a divorce. That their daughter isn't to blame. That only he is. That she had done her utmost, sacrificed her future…'

Eyes wide open and aflame, Manda now wailed:

'What future? What sacrifice? Yallah!'

She stumbled over to the sofa, where she began to cuddle one of the many cushions. The Inspector had enough.

'Must go. See you in court tomorrow at 2 pm. Sharp. A piece of advice: little make-up. A knee-length dress. No shades. Also, be prepared: Adriana's ferocious and her mother will be fierce in her support. Your lover, pseudo-husband, whatever, will duck responsibility. Archi as you call him is well-meaning but weak. Not an unusual combination in my experience. Be strong for two … well, for three. Eat something. You've lost weight.'

She hugged him goodbye.

He liked her perfume. In the cab back home, he realised it reminded him of that unpleasant Penelope piece of work. Also of her daughter Adriana, come to think of it.

Same scent. Foxy architect.

***

TRANSCRIPTS FROM COURT, Monday September 28th.
The facts were stated by the judge: Adrian Jones, a seven-year-old son born out of wedlock but recognized by his father [Etc. Etc.] had been found drifting close to the shore in Margaret's Bay, Dover, Kent, at 7 pm on September 14th, 1997.

Had his drowning been an accident, as the defence posited?

Miss Adriana Jones, adopted daughter of the above-cited father, claimed responsibility for the deed (on the grounds of rage against her not exactly half-brother, comma, and also at the prospect of her Penelope and Neil Jones's, comma, breakup, too painful to endure). Adrian had been an excellent swimmer and the sea, a mirror. Bruises on the boy's neck indicated strangulation, full stop.

According to a local drunk, a blonde teenager had been spotted strolling on the beach in a wetsuit. Maybe two: one tends to see double, does one not?

Great witness.
Prosecutor's opening statement:

This murder, let's call a crime a crime, was premeditated. Miss Adriana Jones followed her adoptive father and discovered that he had a son by Manda D. The victim. Having established this, she had observed the parallel family's – yes, I insist on calling it that – habits. For weeks, disguised as an ice-cream vendor (affidavits from witnesses E, D and F), she trapped Ms Terenski, Adrian's governess, into a near-unconscious condition: the woman suffered from diabetes. Milk + sugar rendered her unable to keep a vigilant eye on the boy.

Thirteen years old or not, the prosecution went on to argue, the teenager's behaviour was akin to that of a cerebral, calculating adult. A helpless, hurt child? Come again.

'May I remind my learned colleague,' the defence counsel, hitherto supressing yawns, counter-argued with a jolt of energy, 'that adolescents have long ago ceased being kids? And point out that my client, yet another who has fallen prey to the plague of absentee parents, had spent most of the ten years prior to this … drama, on her own. Immersed, er, in mystery novels. In a welcoming home, or what she clung onto as its symbol, but alone all the same. There was staff, granted, in that house, but their responsibilities did not include the care of the child. Seems Miss Adriana rejected any such care.'

Readjusting his wig and wiping his forefront, the counsel proceeded:

'Though the psychological assessment isn't incumbent upon me – Dr Tontow will soon be asked to take the stand – a traumatised young person's imagination [here, a reminder of her sad origins] was bound to drift into murky waters.'

Short cough.

'Sorry. Allow me to rephrase – to drift into meanders totally out of her control. In short, the girl lived in a virtual world. Tomorrow's plague, if I may…'

The judge, having finished what the Inspector suspected was a crossword puzzle, slammed down his gavel.

'You may not. As to the subsequent proceedings, I will respectfully entreat you to draw breath in between...'

Some members of the jury smiled. In a drowning case, the vocabulary proved delicate.

'Inspector, please take the stand.'

***

(Back to the yellow pad.)

I said what I have written before, in as telegraphic a style as possible. Starting from the beginning.

Adriana keen to confess, and strikingly unconcerned by the consequences.

Neil and Penelope Jones's cool composure and Manda D's lack of rage, so far as I can tell.

The twice father indulging in double desire – a double life, to simplify. Based on lies. And what are lies, existential lies, turning compulsive, if not diabolic?

(I paused. Wasn't my own life based on binary thinking?)

The problem at hand: my inability to produce reliable eyewitnesses.

On the train to Martin Mill, a dense crowd of kids. On the way back, almost no one – not even a ticket inspector. No CCTVs (in provincial England, these times were yet to come). The police had hung posters at each stop with Adriana's portrait: in vain. The girl had snickered, 'Hey, man, use your brain should it be in working order. I wore a wig several times in order to spy on my Father Dearest, remember? Why would I not do likewise on that infamous Saturday?'

Whereupon I froze.

Hadn't the post-mortem stated the bruises on the boy's indicated more violent pressure on the right side of the neck – facing him – than the other? Had I not noticed, distractedly, yes, but still, that Adriana was left-handed ... meaning it should logically be the other way around, supposing she sat, call it attacked, her prey sitting on top of him?

Summing up: here's a boy winning swimming competitions since kindergarten faced with a frail, possibly anorexic girl in his natural element: the sea. The age difference might be reversed in terms of weight and strength.

With crisp attention, I turned my focus back onto Adriana.

Now standing in the dock, wearing a tennis dress, she was positively glowing. (The girl had never lifted a racket in her life, according to the Scotland Yard file.)

Adriana was enjoying the whole thing. She was the centre of attention. No freak anymore. The heroine of a crime story. No longer its reader.

What bespectacled Doctor Tontow, his luxuriant guardsman's moustache quivering, seemed to recite, exacerbated my discomfort. He banged on about how lonely the born orphan – this in a failed attempt to elicit smiles – had been; how she, unable to be accepted at her snobbish school, unable to make friends, hence disconnected from reality, thus retreated into the fantasy world only books afforded her; in other words, ostracised and ... so on (he lost the thread, as had everyone else), in short Adriana was a thirteen-year-old whose perception of things and actions, not to mention social intercourse and ... all that, was damaged. Possibly, probably, he'd have to conduct further examinations.

Jesus. Even Dr Strangelove seemed normal in comparison to the Tontow guy. (Though my Spanish is rudimentary, it so happens I know the word *tonto* to mean cretin.)

***

No sooner were the proceedings adjourned, the Inspector rushed back to the precinct, the girl's ironic smirk haunting him.

Might the nanny be the key? If nobody else could, he would find Ms Terenski. Illegal papers or not, she could not have disappeared altogether. Especially suffering from diabetes, meaning prescriptions, insulin injections, whatever.

He looked up all physicians listed in Soho and in Dover.

On impulse, he also looked up Sir Duff, the oil tycoon and art collector also known – or so it was rumoured – for having sheltered the infamous Lord Lucan in a windmill he owned above Margaret's Bay, converted into a jewel of a country house. (Lord Lucan, a notorious gambler, more often than not drunk, or broke, or both, had fascinated the Inspector in the mid-seventies when the colourful cavalier had hit the headlines. Suspected to have murdered his kids' nanny – having mistaken her, it was assumed, for his wife.)

Nannies! Wives! People!

Heading down the M2 to Dover he wondered: other than Neil (in Switzerland at the time of the drowning) and Adriana (insisting she'd been there) who had been around?

Other than Ms Terenski – Manda. But Manda was no Medea.

Possibly due to an exhaustion compounded by the heavy traffic, he chuckled. His journey along that particular road was slower than it took the Duke of Wellington to ride to

Walmer Castle, changing horses at Canterbury, a hundred and fifty years before.

Yes. Experience had often confirmed the beeline to be no shortcut. More poignantly, it oftentimes raised the ominous questions: do truth and certitude, or, for that matter, justice and the law, bear much correlation to one another?

The Inspector did find the nanny, registered under yet another false name, in the Red Owl Inn, reputed for its excellent food and eccentric owner. He also spotted Algernon Duff. Both sat at a corner table enjoying what looked like a gargantuan meal. The improbability of coincidence, again and again.

Sir Duff had repeatedly been lampooned by the yellow press for his taste in women. Hold on! Not suggesting he had a crush on the old lady. But exotic ones such as Manda...

Introductions cut short, the public servant told the dashing gentleman how he hated driving, his job, and pub food.

Duff laughed good-heartedly and ordered a crispy duck.

This intermezzo proved most enjoyable even though it led nowhere, really.

***

In court the following day, Penelope brandished a sheet of blue paper.

'Intercepted this morning,' she hissed. 'Signed by Manda.'

'New exhibits aren't admissible unless...'

She ignored the judge and, at the pitch of her voice, read:

My Lover, no longer my saviour.

– but not forgotten. Denounce my devotion if you must. Describe my double personality if you want I don't care.

Erotic, bordering on sadomasochistic prose followed, once again and once too much.

The Inspector observed Adriana. Not a blink. Then Penelope. How could she inflict such words upon a thirteen-year-old? Her voice made steady and steely by malice, she went on.

'I'm writing this on my knees on them I live. You're my poison, I'm your blood. What happened to Adrian…'

Manda fainted. An ambulance was called for.

'How dare you?' boomed the judge, shooting an incensed glance at no one in particular. 'This court is in recess until further notice.'

The jury scrambled out in disorder. Before heading toward the door himself, he caught sight of Penelope and Adriana. Tightly intertwined, the Inspector was reminded of a candle, their bodies the stem, their blonde hair the flame. They seemed in prey to spasms. Laughter or sobbing?

Neil? Nowhere in sight.

Later, chilled to his bones while ambling along the Thames Embankment as joggers and dog-walkers roamed, he promised himself he'd avoid them. Alliterations.

Had Manda really written these lines? It reeled of déjà entendu.

An investigation is like the editing of a film, he mused. You must bring coherence to piecemeal, seemingly disconnected sequences. It's all about continuity. To establish the latter, you need experience – combined with an imagination police officers are asked to harness.

A surge of adrenalin kicked in. Soon thereafter, its exact reverse: dispirited, he felt as if his feet were attached to iron chains.

Concrete? Iron? An hour later, his head aching, the Inspector sat up in his bed. No. Everything seemed abstract. Including the counsel's semi-detached attitude. Might they also have been struck by the fact that whole plot presented far too many cracks to hold water … hmm. His own emotions were smelting. Was he to chide himself for it?

The Joneses, Adriana, Manda … all were lying. By omission, by permission or by – the word eluded him. Barefaced lies. The one and only consistent person, from the start, had been: Penelope.

***

The nanny had agreed to testify. Though in a critical state of diabetes, her vision more often than not blurred, as oftentimes was her memory, and with her cognitive faculties dwindling, she came across as genuine. Yet: what did she add to the evidence? Pretty little other than goodwill. Indeed, she had been spoken to on various occasions by a person, young according to her voice, who asked questions such as what's the boy's name, how old, would you like an ice-cream – stuff like that. Might she identify the voice?

'Don't think so. People talk to me all the time. I mean either in real life or in my recollections.'

'Could you describe the person who spoke to you on Saturday the 14th?'

'Are we still in September? Oh my gosh.'

The judge dismissed Ms Terenski as a dotty spinster. The Inspector wasn't too sure.

The one thing she mumbled of any interest had pertained to how Manda, though a great parent, was immature. How Adrian acted more protectively, in many ways, than his mother. Rather peculiar, come to think of it.

'Think no more,' Dr Tontow pontificated. 'The term is personality disorder. Mother and son had, to put it simply, suffered from and tended to…'

The judge was, by now, snoring. As to the jury, they were watching their watches or nothing at all.

Why, pray, would he admit that he'd turned his binoculars in the direction of one little house, reminding him of a painting by Matisse, where he would admire a woman reminiscent of an Orientalist model?

'Let me point out, esteemed Inspector, how much trouble I got into because of my friendship with Lord Lucan. Besides. On that particular Saturday I was playing cricket with my friend Sam Carton, miles away.'

***

(Back to the yellow pad – would it end in the wastepaper basket, as so many of its predecessors?

By now, I merely dotted down fragments of the proceedings. I longed for all this to be over. Deserved a holiday. To Morocco, perhaps.)

'Objection!'

'Withdrawn, Your Honour.'

'I stand corrected. Not captivated, if I…'

'You may not.'

'No leading questions!'

'So long as my learned colleague refrains from parading hearsay…'

And so on. Exculpatory and incriminating evidence cancelling each other out; one sustained; the other overruled. Cross-examinations? There weren't many. Relevance?

Adriana, let's not forget, never retracted her guilty plea.

Both the prosecution and the defence hadn't seemed to give much of a damn from the start. It had been pouring with rain for almost a week. Many historians claim that the first 1917 Russian Revolution would never have erupted had the weather not been unusually lenient that very February, vindicating Montesquieu's climate theory – not relevant here either, agreed.

I also dozed off. In my half-slumber, I pictured:

ME: You should be the defendant. Salacious parallel lives. Cheating across the line. Wanting to have it both ways, each leading to a DEAD end. Had you come clear, had you opted for one woman or the other, for one existence as opposed to its negative – if you will allow a photographic metaphor – you might well have avoided a tragedy. Saved a life. Your son's for one – not to mention Manda's.

NEIL JONES: How would you know? So I yielded to double desire. What prevents you from doing the same? You, wallowing in frustration, disenchanted with your professional life, unfulfilled as a playwright? Get real!

ME: How dare you?

NEIL JONES: It's all about equations, sir. An architect is good at solving problems of balance, weight and counterweight, all that. Now look at you. Equilibrium is a matter of discipline.

ME: Where did your much vaunted geometrical mind get you? To guilt by proxy. Just as well you were in Switzerland on that Saturday… Moral culprits aren't sentenced to lifelong imprisonment – but to a life of remorse.

NEIL JONES (smiles benignly): Says you. On the grounds of your tediously emphasised experience? Had you conducted a thorough investigation, you'd have discovered that Penny had been driving Adriana to St Margaret's bay on numerous occasions. She had known.

ME: (gaping): What?

NEIL JONES: Yes.

ME: Since when?

NEIL JONES: A while.

ME: Meaning?

NEIL JONES: Being under no obligation to answer, I shall not. Use your brain. Lacking that, common sense, or lacking that too, your imagination. Your choice is your gamble, as...

***

The defence had finally caught on to the left- vs. right-hand implications, invoking the coroner's report, etc. Reducing the case to one of hearsay, it was argued that sorrow and trauma (Dr Tontow's expert opinion) didn't justify the accusation, nor corroborate a capricious confession. 'No vicarious revenge, no restitution, I add for your wise guidance,' the psychiatrist had concluded. As usual, his words eluded comprehension.

Adriana was acquitted. Reasonable doubt. Mental irresponsibility. Technicalities. As trials so often boil down to.

The jury's opprobrium seemed directed at Manda. She should have been more vigilant: where had she been on that Saturday afternoon in September? Frolicking with her lover, a married man? Did the letter uncouthly read out in court not indicate the victim's mother's craving, a pathological need for punishment?

The architect was treated as collateral damage. A limping toy in the hands of two strong-willed women, he had first been manoeuvred into fatherhood; now into mourning. His countenance was nothing short of admirable.

Penelope? Protective of her adopted daughter, neither permeable to provocation nor prone to a loss of self-control, she was yet another victim, understandably vindictive.

Case closed. Jury dismissed with thanks.

One hell of a denouement, sighed the Inspector.

Were he to epilogue this experience one day, he would describe:

… how Adriana's pout, from petulant, became sulky;

… how Neil Jones, as white as the Cliffs of Dover, had rasped something under his breath, then thrown his head back and kept it so, before tipping over and vomiting;

… how Penelope's mother, who had slithered into court looking pink from head to toe, patted Adriana's shoulder, only to be spitefully rebuffed;

…. how, as all attendants scrambled to their feet, Penelope had clasped the judge's hands and how the latter had winked with lecherous eyes;

… and how Manda, darting a glance so charged with bewilderment and hatred at Penny Jones that it would have petrified the woman (busy wiping her sunglasses, her body language triumphal) had pulled out a razor blade.

4

WHY NOT?

I

The plane from Paris to Barcelona had reached its cruising altitude.

'Other than flying, nothing scares me!' the platinum blonde next to me sighed. 'Oh well. So what?'

The captain, gleefully announcing he had just recovered from cataract surgery, said we might arrive ahead of schedule.

'Really,' she moaned sarcastically. 'And how did his hand amputation go?'

'Time will tell...'

'Don't mention time!' she shot back, looking like one who'd seen the devil. 'In exactly one week, my biological clock will tick into the ominous forties. The fact that my financial portfolio is following the same trend stands of little consolation. I have all I need except true love. D'you know Shakespeare's sonnet of the same name?'

An answer seemed redundant.

'Who cares? Although no heiress in the Guggenheim or Agnelli league, poetry's a luxury I indulge in, even though cultural lacunae are all the rage in my golden cage. There's only so much memory you can store, right? Want a drink?'

'No. Thanks.'

She now faced me, a cheeky look on her face.

'Sorry. Had a few back at the airport. Drinking stops my brain – or what's left of it – from spinning. Or is it focusing? Never mind. Twenty years of useless overload from the best education plus a mother who made me learn telephone directories by heart – and here goes! Scatter-braininess. Classical rebound.'

Listening to her was like watching a play you're not interested in with no fire exit in sight.

'Yes. I fell in and out of love. Travelled around, buying then reselling houses. Who? Where? I forget to remember. Suddenly, it's now.'

No answer forthcoming, she carried on:

'The eclectic lot I call friends, mainly drinking compan-ions with whom to share hang-ups, find me amusingly fickle. Worrying, wouldn't you say?'

I opened my book.

'Actually, I don't resent spongers, so long as they play with hands too busy taking to contemplate cheating. Better a scoundrel with a heart than a preacher without scruples. Right?'

I finally turned to her, burying any hope of silence. The woman's face bore a vague resemblance to Julie Christie – as did her voice. Beguiling yet vulnerable.

'Whoever envies the image is short-sighted. Behind it, I've always been a mess. When making love, I'm unable to surrender. When I offer presents, the recipient's gratitude is my foremost motivation. The bottom line? I'm an emotional cripple.'

Words like these would have made me jump had I been able to. In my present condition, I often wish I could unscrew my head and kick it afar; but whilst alive, I'm no longer kicking. Now, that stranger telling me about her poor little rich girl's plight!

'Approaching my fatidic birthday, the panic of having missed out on the essential sneaks in. Is my past made of nothing but baleful digressions tessellated at random? Christ, is nothing, or no one, good enough? What more do I want other than everything?'

Just as I was about to ask for a change of seat, she unexpectedly and gently touched my arm.

'D'you live in Barcelona?'

'Yes.'

'On your own?'

'More than less.'

After her tiresome monologue, in the best English, granted, if a bit ornate, the woman looked away.

'Recently, a lawyer friend, much older than I, yet light years younger in some ways, reappeared out of the blue. We've known each other since my student years. He proposed a modus vivendi. The idea? "You're alone, so am I. We're both surrounded by lots of people, mostly for the entertainment value. You have wealth and looks, I have wit and knowledge. Good team."'

She laughed. I did not. Lawyers had robbed me of my last financial resources.

'Told him that I still hope for more than an arrangement,' she continued. 'Extraordinary how harsh words, uttered in a kind voice, distort men's egos. They won't believe the truth delivered without drama. Anyway. Standing by my flat's bay windows, watching the Louvre cast its flood-lit silhouette over the Seine, I often feel that splendour exacerbates melancholy.'

This must have reminded her of herself for she pulled out her powder compact and threw an inquisitive look into the mirror.

'Did you know that the second-highest suicide rate among adolescents, after ghastly places like Siberia, used to be on Capri? The discrepancy between overpowering beauty and fading expectations is a killer. Am I drifting? I'd better stick to burgundy.'

Having summoned the stewardess, she removed her cardigan. *Why drink and drive if you can snort and fly?* was embroidered on the T-shirt she wore underneath. Capturing my glance, she giggled.

'I do the lot. Why not? No children to worry about. What could I offer a kid except a muddled life in a lopsided world? Nor do I want to live long enough to become a has-been. Although (she added in a tone that sounded more sincere than anything so far) I wish I could find out who really cares for me – beyond the visible reasons, that is.'

Astonishing woman. For some vague reason, it was hard not to like her.

'Who do *you* care about?' I ventured, forgoing any chance of reading.

'What? Oh. Whom? I'm not so sure anymore. Unless it's the other way round… Do you?'

Life had decided for me, changing my perspective in

ways I'd rather not have known. Coupling mine onto her train of thought, thoughts being my main vehicle these days, a quaint idea dawned upon me. Fiction has become my refuge. I shrugged.

'Why not create a situation that would help you sort out who's around for what, and why?'

She didn't even blink.

'Funny you should say that. I've thought of it on occasions but it didn't seem an option someone used to complicated people in comfortable situations would choose. By the way: what's your name?'

'Sandra.'

'Mine's Ines.' She extended a warm hand. 'French with Spanish origins.'

She then sunk into deep thoughts, or so it seemed, as she didn't talk for at least three minutes.

'Sandra? May I ask you something?'

'What?'

'Would you teach me how to move in a wheelchair? I could then pretend to be, well ... confronted with the same ordeal that you face every day. Quite a test situation, wouldn't you say?'

My astonishment was such that I didn't react.

'The cardigan falling on the floor, remember? My picking it up. See?'

She looked me in the eyes – into both eyes at once, a rare gift; then asked, 'How did it happen?'

'A car crash seven years ago.'

We were starting our descent to Barcelona. Ines grew livid.

'Please let me hold onto your arm. I'm frightfully scared when planes land.'

Since when had someone asked me for help?

II

At the airport – pushing my chair, no protest accepted – she pursued her questioning.

'Oxbridge accent and all, why do you live here rather than in Surrey or something like that?'

Astonishing, for I indeed had been brought up in Surrey. What Ines lacked in terms of tact her instinct made up for.

'Barcelona, since the Olympics in 1992, is the best city for disabled people in Spain. After my accident, was there much alternative to Southern Europe? If you can't do much, it might at least be outdoors. Sparky skies chase inner gloom. Besides, my husband was Catalan. Spanish people are very human. Only the expression *minusvalidos*, minus-valid, isn't.'

Ines giggled.

'It's too awful not to be funny. Sorry Sandra.'

Disconcerted by my manoeuvre to forgo support, she took my hands in hers.

'May I suggest … no offence meant...'

'What?' Impatience nearly made me lose my bearings.

Ines observed the scene with the look of someone who has nothing to lose – not because she had it all: she looked forlorn. She reminded me of a child planning some mischief and being rejected. That was the thing about her: overconfidence coupled with insecurity. All at once.

After a slight hesitation, she took a gamble.

'Sandra. Here's the idea. You call my eager admirers and my supposedly best friend; explain that I had an accident the consequences of which could be permanent and hint

I need company. Then we wait. See who'll turn up, who'll say what, who'll cope – and how.'

More than outraged, I was startled. What kind of a proposal was that? Just as well she hadn't called it a deal and … a distraction.

Didn't it cross her candidly egoist mind how perverse this might become to all involved? The situation reminded me of a picture I had painted before the accident. It depicted a fragmented shadow leaning against a slanted pillar. Was a metaphor coming true? A sinuous thought.

On the other hand – had I not planted the seeds of such a scheme in her mind with my flippant remark – meant to divert her attention from me?

I couldn't help feeling amused though. It had been too long since something unexpected had happened to me.

And so I answered: 'Why not?' Why not – the two words that often taunt one's destiny.

Ines clapped her hands and, having insisted she drop me off in her car, now insisted on accompanying me to my flat.

After a look at the view (council flats) and at my antiques (valuable), she asked:

'Why two wheelchairs?'

'In case of punctures that we, of course, cannot fix. Were I a 'tetra', I would need a plastic one to take into the shower as a support. My second, in aluminium, is almost four times as expensive as the heavy steel chair provided by social security. Alas, it's broken.'

'How much does it cost?'

I told her.

'Christ! The price I pay for two Botox injections!'

Inhale, exhale, oooohm, I told myself.

'And the kitchen!' she exclaimed. 'I bet kids love your

place! Everything at their eye level, like in a puppet house!'

Had Ines not been Ines, I would have freaked. Instead of explaining the obvious, I pointed out that our worst fear is a power cut. We stock lots of supplies, just in case.

'In the bottom cupboards, as you can...'

'Oh dear!' she exclaimed, glancing at her watch, 'must rrrrrrun. But do, Sandra, promise you'll come for lunch tomorrow! Someone will pick you up around two. Please?'

Ines was gone before I could object.

An hour later, the chauffeur was back with a truck-load of flowers. He held a white rose in his hand. 'That's from me, miss. *Hasta mañana.*'

III

The following day, the same guy came to fetch me. It created an embarrassing stir in the neighbourhood.

Lunch in the Hotel Gran Colón's atrium was lavish and Ines, an irresistible mixture of frivolity and empathy. Her sense of humour softened the edges of our different outlooks and rounded the angles of our contrasting sensitivities.

Leaving the dining room, she asked if she could try my chair. Of course, I said. *Le ridicule tue* was unknown to her, or else she'd have been long buried.

I taught her how to slow down, accelerate or stop abruptly. Receptionist and concierge watched Ines driving to and fro with discreet bewilderment.

Ines in a wheelchair with her Hermès coat and high heels was a surreal sight indeed. A sight which made me realise that I had been neglecting my appearance for the wrong reasons. When some recently arrived hotel guest asked whether she needed help, Ines smiled graciously and, instead of looking sullen as I tend to do, beamed.

It was ironic: while she was learning about the troubles we must cope with, I was remembering the privileges left to us.

'Let's go to my suite, shall we?'

Becoming used to her questions requiring no answer, I explained that one has to get into the lift backwards in order to avoid collisions getting out. In the streets, one has to position one's handbag in such a way as to prevent anyone from robbing it.

'How interesting! What about sex?' she winked with both eyes.

That was Ines. No oblique glances.

'The least of my problems,' I lied.

'Poor darling! You know the saying: "A woman without a man is like a fish without a bicycle"?'

She bit her lips. She was no fool.

Back on her feet, she took matters into her hands. Manicure, pedicure and massage organised within minutes. For three hours I was pampered like a doll. It was divine. Then Ines rearranged my hair, put make-up on my face and helped me change into outfits I could no longer afford.

'Small token of my gratitude.'

I wanted to refuse but couldn't – not only because Ines would not take no for an answer, but because luxury felt good. And yes, it was also a treat to feel pretty again. We giggled like teenagers.

Ines was lavishing me with more than she realised and I, for once, had the impression of giving something worthy in return. Call it affection. Yes. She inspired it.

Time flew – and that was the best of it all, for it was another sensation long forgotten.

'I have too much of it,' Ines said while ordering club sandwiches.

'Do you have hobbies? A passion?'

'Where I come from, Sandra, girls dabble around when not becoming career women. Actually, in between divorces, I was a well-known fashion columnist. But I became bored. I easily do. Needing some outlet for my energy, I wrote a book about the rag world. A kind of outsider's inside story. No good – I knew a lot but described it badly. I had met plenty of stars out of orbit, no doubt, but lacked the malice expected by yellow-press readers. The book was savaged by the critics.'

Ines's eyes started welling with tears. Her lavish alcohol consumption played some part in that.

'I never achieved anything, never loved any man more than three weeks, three months or three years… A fraud and a failure, darling, that's what I am. What the hell do I know about others? What have I done for anyone? Are they too remote, or is it me? I'm a spoilt kid aged forty. That's all.'

She curled into an embryonic position.

'What about you? You never tell me anything!'

'How could I? You do all the talking!'

'Hmm. That's another problem … the main one?'

'Who cares?' I teased, imitating her.

IV

'Tell me about your accident.'

I shivered. It had been ages since I agreed to dredge up those bygone days, split into a 'before' and 'after'.

'It occurred right after my husband's funeral. Driving

back to London, too many tears, too little sleep, too much rain… I didn't see the deer ambling down the road. Summed up in a local newspaper: "Ms Sandra Darkins, 33, founder of the prestigious advertising agency NOW, underwent neurosurgery and a bone transplant after a crash on the A23. Considering the gravity of the medullar lesion, her chances of walking again are thin." The rest is crippled me.'

Melodrama wasn't down Ines's street.

'Any reason why a spirited girl like you wouldn't go on working?'

Was there?

'Look,' I defensively replied. 'I became disenchanted with advertising well before Carlos's death. A business exploiting dissatisfaction whilst torpedoing fulfilment? Campaigns, strategy, targets, impact, belligerent lingo… *A crime against humility* is what I nicknamed the sham.'

'Well – isn't that a bit harsh? Or pedantic, for that matter?'

I could have killed the exasperating brat – but she had a point. My very own.

'Quite. But our subconscious is flooded with the notion that what we have isn't good enough, and never will be.'

Whilst I regretted my possibly hurtful words, Ines reflected – without a mirror at arm's length. Quite a feat.

'What did you do, er, afterwards?'

'Learn to play the guitar, to paint, things like that.'

'What about your sentimental life?'

Jesus. Skirt the question?

'Other than my husband, there had been no men in my life. I wasn't going to become a flirt after his death and my accident, was I?'

Leaning against the balustrade with her back turned, she kept silent for quite a while; then asked:

'Do you consider our plan a … distasteful masquerade?'

Our!? Had she even listened to anything I'd said, or had she been, all the while, just thinking about her scheme? Then again. So what?

I looked at my legs – then at Ines. Here was a glamorous woman who 'had it all', men included, at her feet. Was I about to take advantage of her disorientation?

Who was offering what to whom? Was my company making her realise that her problems weren't that serious? Was I recovering confidence thanks to her devil-may-careness? There was something so genuine about Ines that I could not imagine anyone, given the curiosity to scratch the veneer, not being moved by her. I felt far less honest.

'Look, Ines. Since you weigh your self-esteem against the approval and loyalty of others, remember that it's quite simple in the end: those who remain are those who matter.'

She spun abruptly. 'In fairy tales, princes pretend to be frogs. What about heiresses? I can't pretend to be poor, the media having publicised my fortune so widely that every-one knows what I'm worth. To pretend to be ugly would involve surgical stunts. None too pleasant. As to pretend-ing to be deaf or mute, not in my chords at all!'

Latent tension burst like a tyre.

'Are you sure to measure the consequences?'

'That's the very point, isn't it?' she exclaimed. 'Consequences!'

Against my better judgment, I laughed.

'Right! I'll get an extra room and then…'

'No, Ines,' I interrupted peremptorily. 'My own bed is fine.'

'But…'

'No.'

She dared not insist.

V

The following day, the driver made little effort to conceal his surprise upon seeing me roll over the threshold. Had I been 'normal' he might even have whistled. This pleased me no end.

Ines, half an hour later, clapped her hands.

'Sandra! You look like a million dollars!'

Vintage Ines. She wore yet another of her beloved T-shirts. Under the inscription *I'm a work of art* signed Ben, the word '*overrated*' had been stitched on. Ines was a puppy. Money helped, of course. She must have squandered more in twenty-four hours than I spend in a year. To what extent it seduced me I'd rather not dwell upon.

'How many victims today?'

'The lot. You make the calls, pretending you're a nurse or something. Sandra, no grimace! You agreed, remember? Let's get the ball rolling.'

'Shows keep me on the road.'

'You do have a graphic sense of humour!' she chuckled. 'Beware it doesn't become self-complacent! In the long run!'

A surprising remark. It revealed more depth than I would have given Ines credit for. Shame on me. Ines could swing from groove to gravity without batting an eyelid.

'Right,' she said, placing horn-rimmed spectacles on her fine nose and a cigarette in a holder. 'First, my girlfriend Tchach. An interior designer. Though not very bright,

179

hence easy to influence, being let down by her would be the harshest blow of all. Then, the two brothers who've been competing for me for years. Though almost identical in terms of looks, they're psychological opposites. Paul's an artist with a 'Who's Worth How Much' mind. Too bad his social agenda corrupts an outstanding talent! Olivier, on the other hand, is an entrepreneur with an artistic temperament – Richard Branson style, stammer and all. I'm fond of both, Sandra, but have never fallen in love with either. If only they could merge into one!'

She removed her glasses awaiting feedback. Disappointed, she proceeded:

'Where were we? Yeah. Tchach first. Paul and Olivier second. Then the lawyer I told you about. James. Never would he fail me, but still... Finally Konstantin, Koni, my second ex-husband. An architect. We shared tumultuous times – until five years ago. Last May he resurfaced, claiming never to have ceased loving me. Truth is that his kids had married and, all of a sudden, he needed me again since they didn't need him anymore. Another classic.'

I picked up the receiver.

'Good afternoon. May I please talk to Miss Tchach Scotuli?'

'Who may I say is calling?' answered a polished voice.

'The Clinic Sofia in Barcelona.'

'Concerning? ... Oh ... Mrs Ines Escudo?'

Only seconds later a breathless voice asked:

'What's the matter? Anything happened to Ines?'

'I'm afraid so. An accident. We operated all night. She'll get through but she might end up paraplegic. Her head was gravely injured, meaning neurological side effects, I won't...'

'Para-what?'

'Paralysed from the waist down.'

Silence.

'Anything I can do?'

'Well, the lady having asked us to inform you in case of complications, we imagine it would be of great comfort if you could pay her a visit.'

'When?'

'The sooner the better. It's a difficult shock to assimilate on one's own... She's presently recovering from heavy anaesthetics but should be fully conscious by this evening.'

'I'll book tomorrow's first available flight. Please give my secretary the clinic's address.'

I did, except it was the hotel's. Handed a substantial tip, the Gran Colón's concierge received instructions with philosophical aloofness (acquiring a wheelchair had been the latest).

That her closest girlfriend didn't ask questions left me pensive. People who care usually want to know exactly what happened. On the other hand, what more can a person do other than leap on a plane?

I repeated the exercise with the two brothers, who shared a house in Paris. The one I talked to was Olivier, the artistic entrepreneur.

'God ah – Almighty!' he exclaimed. 'What's wrong?'

Same story.

'Un ... unfortunately there's a, er, business trip to Italy I cannot poss, possibly cancel, so it'll be in a few days. Ah – can I help?'

'Well ... perhaps inform your brother who, according to names she gave us before the op, is also a close friend of Mrs Escudo.'

'Will, er, do. Thanks for calling.'

I surmised Olivier would not tell Paul. Stammer or not, he sounded like a man of resolute character.

Next, the ex-husband who had professed eternal love. My little speech no sooner over, he barked:

'In a meeting. Can't talk. Got your number stored. Will call back.'

The line went dead. That was snappy. Yet I fathomed that Koni would the first to turn up. You develop highly strung vibes when deprived of other faculties.

The next call was to James. Ines, who'd been listening to the conversations on the loudspeaker, relaxed.

'Hulloooo?'

I went through what was becoming routine.

'Who operated?'

I named the surgeon I knew.

'Please put me on.'

'Impossible, sir.'

'Then ask him to call me.'

'Well…'

This was getting tricky. Ines gestured I should pretend to be able to connect her.

'Would you like to speak to Mrs Escudo?'

'Absolutely!' he boomed.

Ines took on a bedroom voice. No trouble with that…

'Hulloooo my darling?' she crooned.

'Are you all right?'

'Alive.'

'Would you like me to come over?'

'My dearest, there isn't much you can do right now except interfering with doctors who would resent it. Don't worry.'

'Fine,' he answered a little too readily.

Ines averted my searching glance.

'Toodleoo then. Call you tomorrow.'

'Excellent,' she murmured demurely.

James hadn't asked for the clinic's name.

VI

In the same situation but for real, I had harboured few illusions. Unlike Ines, I had never been worshipped for my wealth. In an unremarkable way, I had earned lots of money but nothing comparable to the fortune that had fallen into her lap at birth. When, surmounting inhibitions, I finally brought myself to tell a few friends about what lay in store for me, their silence, even worse than their absence, had deepened the chasm between me and 'the others'. But then: after years of selling beauty and health, how was I to expect sympathy for its antithesis? My hunch had proven right, with few exceptions. In addition Carlos, my husband, was always rather antisocial, and I had lost touch with many relations. Indifference shouldn't have surprised me, I reasoned, my heart cringing.

'You know what, Sandra? Must go to the hairdresser's. Nothing like it to chase the blues. Want to come?'

In response to my curt 'No,' I half-expected some cheeky admonition on the lines of 'Don't you consider back-pedalling!' Impossible to decipher that woman.

'Here's a list of DVDs. Choose whatever you fancy, will you – please?'

Before sauntering out, she asked:

'Like my lipstick?'

'Nice,' I remarked distractedly.

'Good.'

Bouquets started arriving.

First, white lilies and roses. Tchach's note said: 'Sweet school friend, I'm shattered by the dismal news. Will come as soon as poss, frenzy allowing... The bottom of my soul overflows with thoughts and wishes. Let me call tomorrow. Love from your FF.'

'Forever Friend' explained Ines, contemplating her cherry hair-streaks made to match lipstick and nail polish. 'Invented in boarding school ... has it reached its expiry date, I vaguely wonder? Anyway, how nice!'

'Indeed,' I echoed with equally tepid conviction.

A more exuberant bouquet arrived. The note was short: 'Shall arrive tomorrow 10:45 am. At 5 pm to Madrid and from there to Milano. Be brave, *mon trésor*. Olivier.'

No mention of Paul.

'Poor darling! Changed all his plans! Shit, I feel guilty.'

'Too late, *querida*.'

My hospital room hadn't turned into a botanical garden. She should bloody well face the music, I couldn't help thinking. Sensing my irritation, she addressed me with her brightest Colgate smile.

'Sorry, Sandra. Time for a drink.'

Another knock on the door. This time, no flowers, just a note handed on a tray by a young bellboy. 'In the lobby. Nice clinic. What's going on? Konstantin.'

Ines turned as white as chalk.

'He must have chartered a private plane,' she muttered. Events were getting out of hand for someone so used to calling the shots.

'Get ready. I'll handle the preliminaries.'

Opening the door of the suite, I almost collided with a

handsome man looking far younger than mid-fifties.

'Name's Koni. Who are you?' he enquired, staring at the chair.

'A friend. Well ... a nurse become a friend.'

'Good,' he answered warmly. 'Where's Ines?'

'Probably...'

'How bad is it?'

'Nobody can tell. She might be able to walk again. She might not.'

'When was the surgery?'

'Three days ago. Same osteologist as mine. He let her discharge herself from hospital prematurely. You know how she gets when she wants something...'

'I certainly do.'

Ines wheeled into the drawing room looking fabulous. (So did the chair, fitted with a fine ebony seat and bleached woven strand-cane, aaargh...)

Too much sex makes you short-sighted decreased in size towards the plunging V-neck. The ex-husband smiled.

'Wish I needed glasses.'

'What did you expect?'

'Dinner.'

Confused, she threw me a worried glance.

'Only if Sandra comes along because you see...'

'... I did mean the both of you,' said Koni, throwing me the kind of look no man had for years.

Down we went, Ines getting into the lift backwards as I had taught her, and her ex, clever enough not to help.

There was a cosy Italian restaurant near the hotel. Koni chatted away. Ines was in great spirits, which left me wondering why she had to put him to the test. The man obviously adored her. He was explaining that he had already given instructions for his house to be fitted out with ramps should she wish to stay there for as long as she wanted. After declaring that life in a chair can be very fulfilling when endowed with imagination and talent, an abrupt change from platitudes, an abrupt change of repertoire:

'Ines, I'm submitting a bid to build a village for the disabled near Milan. Do come along. Not tomorrow, obviously, but in about two weeks, when my chances will need a boost. Yes?'

Was she thinking what I couldn't help wondering? That Koni, however genuine his devotion, pictured himself as the do-gooder with Ines as a feminine Christopher Reeves on the podium by his side? Ines's body language betrayed nothing. Then she unexpectedly burst out laughing.

Smooth like velvet and with an irony he didn't, or perhaps did, perceive, she riposted: 'Wonderful! How uplifting to feel useful despite ... everything.'

'Done deal then!'

The man coughed, glanced at his watch and announced his plane was waiting. Ines smiled disarmingly.

'Sandra will make sure I get back safely. Don't worry.'

He didn't seem to. The meeting was over. Leaving a huge tip, he kissed us both on the forehead and was gone.

Ines's smile dropped like a handkerchief you stop waving.

'People who give usually want something in return, right?'

'Just as well you see it this way.'

'Quite. Anyway, let's catch some sleep. Don't forget Olivier is turning up tomorrow morning!'

'I must go home.'

'No,' she cried. 'I've arranged for a room with a communicating door. Please don't go.'

The begging tone from the lady who had it all made me uneasy.

'I must fetch clothes and stuff, Ines.'

'Taken care of.' She repeated 'Please!'

I hesitated. My muddled conscience whispered, 'Why not yield to a plea which, after seven years of hardship, is also an excursion into a world where all things become easy at once?' It then whispered back, 'careful...'

'Okay,' I heard myself answer.

'Oh Sandra! Wonderful!'

I found a silk gown spread on the bed, and a lovely, knee-length dress. Knee-length...Beside the toothbrush and paste, a make-up kit had been left near the washbasin, a face-peeling mask and all, plus cream and scent by Guerlain. A fortune's worth of goodies.

VII

The next morning, she sailed into 'my' room out of breath, wearing a jogging suit.

'All swell an' groovy but gotta send an SMS to Olivier explaining I was granted leave from the hospital,' she chirped.

A trolley with exotic fruit, scrambled eggs and toast materialised.

'We need strength,' Ines declared.

'When do you expect the guy?'

'Around noon. Anything you'd like to do until then?'

'Nothing, Ines, and on my own.'

'You're a pain,' you know that? See you later!' she added cheerfully, walking out with a peach in one hand and a cigarette in the other.

I had a bubble bath and a beauty session from head to toe. It had been a long, long time since I had been able to touch my legs without looking the other way.

Upon reappearing, she wore a T-shirt depicting a dilapidated castle with the caption: *Wealth is no longer a sin – it's a miracle.*

'The same trousers again?'

'*Querrrida*! People like me buy what they fancy five times instead of one!'

'What was I thinking?'

The phone rang. Olivier had arrived ahead of time.

'What shall we do?'

'Improvise!'

The concierge, who had seen Ines rush up the stairs an hour ago and now watched her extricating herself from the lift in a wheelchair, did not alter his demeanour one iota. She addressed him with an expensive smile.

A man who must have been more or less our age came forwards, a parcel in one hand, a mobile telephone in the other. He moved like a cat, and his amber-coloured eyes reminded me of one.

'Bonjour beautiful!'

Olivier tossed a rather curt 'hello' at me.

'Who's, er, she?' he whispered.

'My friend Sandra. I'm already out of hospital thanks to her intervention.'

'Can we t-talk alone?'

'Why? I've told her all about my life … my former life,' she added, looking at her feet demurely.

'All right, um … then. I have a lim, a limousine waiting, specially fitted… Let's go to the harbour and, and have some tapas. Fine?'

She softly squeezed my hand.

'Very much,' she replied.

It was good to sit in the mild October sun. Olivier ordered mineral water and Coke Light, *calamares fritos, jabugo* ham with *pimientos*, asking neither of us what we wanted. While they exchanged trivialities, I watched the fishermen spreading their nets, young mothers pushing their prams, children playing. Was this Sunday? When staying at the Gran Colón, time gets blurred.

The conversation lingered. Olivier fiddled with the knot of the parcel leaning against his chair.

'A p-present from Paul.'

'What is it?' Ines squeaked.

'Open it!'

It was a portrait in red chalk of her and seemed to have been cut at the waist and reframed.

'How lovely,' she murmured, genuinely enraptured.

It was a damn good drawing.

'How is he?'

'E, er, engaged,' answered the brother.

'Oh! Whom to?'

'A friend of … of yours, er. Tcha, um – called Tchach.'

'Really?' Ines half choked. 'She isn't a friend! She's my closest friend! Why didn't she tell me?'

'S, search me,' Olivier shrugged. 'All I know is he, well, she, er they met the, three weeks ago and, um, the wed, the wedding's in ten days.'

'That's how it should be,' retorted Ines, high-pitch again. 'People do waste too much time, wouldn't you say? *Carpe diem* and all that. Three weeks, three years: there's always a three involved in points of no return or should I say, of missed u-turns.'

Powdering her nose, she asked Olivier what was new in his life.

'Not much. I have le, left the house to Paul and found a, er... kind of loft overlooking the Ch, Champs de Mars. You'll see it soon.'

'If the lift's big enough!'

'There isn't ... one,' he blushed.

I rolled away, pretending to need exercise.

What happened thereafter, no idea. About twenty minutes later, Ines caught up with me, her eyes a double-barrelled shotgun. 'So much for that creep,' she declared. 'Can you believe that he never stopped fiddling with his shoelace after you left!?'

Did the fiddling annoy her more than the news of Paul and Tchach's impending marriage? Not impossible.

We spent some time wheeling around aimlessly, I enjoying the early autumn's iridescent light and the iodine-filled breeze, Ines noticing neither. If she felt humiliated – one guy offers her a deal; the next is sent by the third as a messenger to announce a breach of trust and friendship – she never let it transpire.

'He had the decency of leaving us the car.'

'Still enjoying this?'

She faced me with these disarming eyes of hers.

'Don't know. Am I overstretching your patience?'

'Well...'

'A surprise. You're coming to Monte Carlo with me!'

Off she raced in her wheelchair. When I reached the car she was sitting in it, smoking delectably. I, on the other hand, fumed with indignation.

'Dilapidating money doesn't entitle you to boss me around!'

Had I slapped her hard, her face couldn't have shown more pain. We remained silent for a long while. Then I got into the car.

'Forgive me,' she murmured, wrapping a shawl around my shoulders, clasping my hand in hers.

VIII

'Nice outing, Milady?'

'Positively splendid,' smiled Ines.

'I took the liberty of signing for a DHL delivery on your behalf,' continued the groomed concierge. 'Awaiting you upstairs. Are we racing up or rolling into the lift, Madam?'

'The lift,' answered Ines with a graceful swirl.

Once in the drawing room, she stretched her legs with a sigh of relief.

'Christ! Don't think I could stand that much longer!'

Bitch! But then, head in her hands, she collapsed into a huge armchair, looking frail. I filled two glasses with vodka. She wouldn't drink any of it – a most disquieting development. Instead, she rushed into the bathroom. Sick? It sounded like it.

A big envelope was lying on the console table next to the door. I saw it had been sent by the Hon. James White, QC. I closed my eyes.

When I opened them again, night had fallen. Ines, dressed in turquoise silk pyjamas, was scribbling something at the desk.

'Finally!'

She tore open the envelope and frowned. Inside were two smaller ones. The first contained a cheque with a note saying, 'For the best wheelchair money can buy.' The amount was exorbitant. I could have bought ten new ones with it. Ines handed me the cheque. 'You keep it. It's made out to the bearer.' She added 'Please' with precipitation.

The second envelope contained a hand-written letter. 'May I read it aloud?'

Not waiting for an answer:

My darling Dove. I could not sleep all night, got terribly drunk, felt like a child and like a shit. The image of you dancing or bouncing around, driving like an ace and behaving like an ass haunts me. You have always represented health and energy, temper and passion. You helped me feel young again – in any event, less wasted. You injected joy in my rather cynical life and I loved it. I also needed it. You see, dear Dove, I haven't always been exaggeratedly respectful of property or, for that matter, of the well-being of my fellow souls. In short I specialised in criminal law. I heard so much crying, witnessed so much despair and desolation, not to mention the suicide attempts, that I swore to myself I'd never ever face distress again if it could be avoided. It can. Since the future began, years before we met, I've selected my clients and my acquaintances according to one and the same criteria: happiness – or at least, frivolity.

'That fits,' I mumbled, becoming annoyed. 'Quite an alpha ego, he seems to have. A weak one, paradoxically.'

'Yeah. Plus the most upwardly mobile guy since Icarus. Well, let's hear him out.'

In court I defend stupid rogues, amusing scoundrels, brainless thieves, Mafiosi basking in delusion, and the like. Let me call them people who have no conscience, hence know no remorse, even when parting with substantial fees. A long prelude, I know, to explain this: though immature, I have always been as hard a worker as wild a player. They call me Peter Pan. Some discarded ex or other coined the nickname, and it stuck. That said, darling Dove: not a knave nor a cad enough not to show you the courtesy of being blunt. However, aiding or abetting a person in worse shape than I am? No. You need a fatherly figure. That I cannot provide. Conclusion, my beautiful: could never cope with your plight. Can hardly bear mine. The most difficult thing is never to forget not to remember. Follow me?

Remaining, as always, truly yours —

'Truly yours?' Ha.

'He is truthful, Sandra, let's grant him that.'

Ines opened the window and inhaled deeply. Instead of sobbing, as I half-expected, she burst into laughter.

'He tells me to expect little I don't already have! No line devoid of the first person singular? *Madre*. Dare hope his elocution in court is an improvement on his prose...'

At least he didn't have the effrontery to mention love, I refrained from pointing out. Legs permitting, I would have paced the room like an enraged animal. I had met too many fakes and frauds over the years.

Once that wicked game was over, would mo(u)rning come without warning and take the stars away? No news from her FF, Tchach.

IX

Time had come to do what I had been itching to do.

'Ines, I must call my cousin.'

'Your what?'

'My first cousin and closest relative. He's in Barcelona

for a few days.'

'Why didn't you tell me?'

'We had much on our minds, didn't we?'

'Yes. Me, if that's the hint. Oh well. Tell him to come over!'

I pretended to hesitate.

'He might disapprove of the way you spoil me.'

'Oh *querida*, isn't life complicated enough? Come on! What's he doing in Barcelona?'

'He's here for a shot.'

'A junkie?' chirped Ines.

'A photographer actually.'

'Fashion?'

'Yes.'

'Poor guy. Where does he live?'

'All over the place. For three years he came every third week or so to see me. Don't know what would have become of me had he not.'

When I told Thomas I was having a wonderful time with a new friend, he smiled over the phone.

'Could you meet us?'

'Where?'

'At the Café Lirico on the Ramblas? In an hour?'

'No problem.'

I spent an unusual amount of time in front of the mirror, wondering whether my brother's taste in girls had moved on to post-pubertal.

Down we went in our chairs, Ines intercepting the concierge's oblique glances, me ignoring them.

When my cousin stepped into the Café Lirico, he skidded to a halt.

A few weeks ago, he had seen me in shapeless clothes,

with messy hair and no make-up. Now he recognised the person I had once been. He hugged me with palpable emotion.

'Jesus! Another stunning surprise and you'll provoke a heart attack!'

When Thomas turned to Ines with an outstretched hand, no sound escaped his throat. She said the usual things in her melodious voice with its enticing accent, but also seemed to be having some trouble.

We've all read about 'love at first sight' in prose and in verse, in languages dead and alive, but I, at least, had never seen it first-hand.

Thomas was Ines's type: sporty, lean, dark-haired with light-green eyes. Droopy eyebrows over-lined their kindness. The reciprocal was true. He had always had a foible for Lara in *Doctor Zhivago*. Yet there was more to it but, as one cannot, by definition, describe the ineffable, why try? It felt like an invisible current, an immediate understanding, a shared secret.

'The red hair adds a funky fruity touch,' he teased. 'And cherries, my favourite indulgence!'

Truth is she looked pretty ridiculous, apart from awkward. Why did he find it all endearing? '*Parce que c'etait toi, parce que c'etait moi*'... (Montaigne always comes in handy.)

'I'm so glad,' Thomas stammered. 'Sandra needed a friend to feel alive again.'

'She was the helpful one,' Ines burst out.

However inconsequent their chit-chat, they seemed like two people groping for each other from a distance, exchanging coded signals.

What would Ines do next, I wondered? Lies thrown at

an entourage that well deserved it was one thing; lying to a man who deserved none was another. If trust is the cement of friendship, it is the foundation of love. I knew her well enough by now to surmise that Ines was trying to pierce her emotional maze in search of an answer.

Thomas had recovered a semblance of composure.

'Let's have a little feast.'

Not awaiting an answer (another thing these two had in common) he pushed Ines' chair, with a mischievous, 'Sorry darling, age before beauty!' twinkle in my direction. I wondered if Ines's skin shivered the way mine had the first time my late husband Carlos's hands stroked my hair.

On the way to the Plaza Mayor, Thomas told us about his last three weeks in Buenos Aires working as a photographer for a travel magazine, and how much he had enjoyed getting away from rags and pseudo-stars. (His affairs with models had all ended in boredom and drama.) His birthday only some weeks bygone, he hummed that 'life begins at forty'.

We found an isolated table on a picturesque terrace. Ines almost removed her blazer but thought better of it as underneath, the legend on her T-shirt read: *Why wear a Wonderbra / In the age of Viagra?*

Thomas and Ines talked in a languid, perfectly attuned rhythm. There was magic there and yes, silly as it may sound, I was spellbound.

'Where are you staying by the way?'

Ines was left with no strength for invention.

'The Gran Colón.'

'Nice.'

When we reached the entrance, he asked whether he could come back the following morning and rightly interpreted our silence as a yes.

'Sleep well, my beauties!'

X

Back in the suite, she massaged her neck.

'Anything broken?'

'Sorry?'

'Well, it's called falling in love, is it not...?'

I felt in a good mood. My cousin's compliments had had an uplifting impact. Why had I neglected myself for so long? A facet of self-inflicted self-denial?

'Sandra, I've been thinking,' Ines sighed after a while, inspecting her small feet.

Ines, embarrassed?

'I must tell Thomas that I have put on an act. Yet I cannot tell him why. D'you understand?'

'Of course. Tell him, well ... that you're contemplating writing a play and must transpose yourself into the main character's skin.'

'You figured that out too?'

'Hey! I might not be fully capable anymore, leg-wise, but I still realise that half lies are often better than double truths.'

Ines now looked like a rainbow in the middle of the night.

'One thing, Ines. Call it a warning. Do not hurt my cousin. Please. He's alien to your whims. Don't toy with his heart. It's pretty intact.'

She looked at me with an expression mingling pain with pain.

'I understand your concern. For days you have witnessed

my ability for deception, my hang to narcissism, my pursuit of egotistical aims. Yet. Do you really imagine for one moment that I'm playing right now, with that man's … life? That my former lies will determine…'

'Just frightened. It's your life too.'

She went to the mini-bar and, oh surprise, opened a Coke. After a sip and a grimace, she added rum and repeated the procedure for me.

'Sandra *chérie*, listen. I know one doesn't say 'love at first words' or 'love at first touch', but there was so much more to it than sight. It's almost as if I had, until now, been… the hostage to an absence. Does that sound preposterous?'

No, I answered with a note of sadness.

Thomas and Ines were a born team. They both had a surplus of imagination, a convoluted sense of humour, loads of energy and little self-doubt. Where would that leave me? Alone again?

Next morning, a glorious autumn day, I found Ines pacing the drawing room.

'Didn't sleep a wink.'

'It doesn't show. You need a good breakfast.'

'Not hungry.'

'An unmistakable symptom,' I smiled.

Her lack of repartee was another. I ordered scrambled eggs with bacon and, why not, half a bottle of champagne. New habits take time to die.

The tray appeared after an unusual amount of time, probably due to the waiter's age – a bespectacled, bearded old man who limped in, slightly breathless. Ines jumped to her feet and entreated him not to bother laying it out. 'We'll manage just fine,' she said, slipping him a princely tip.

'Anything else the ladies wish?' his quavering voice asked.

'No,' answered Ines, 'thank you so much.'

As the waiter gasped for air, flinging his right hand to his chest while stumbling towards the door, Ines persuaded him to sit down.

'Can't do that, Ma'am,' the old man heaved. 'I must attend to my duties.'

'No way. You're going to stay right here for as long as it takes for you to feel better. What's the matter with your leg?'

'An injury, Madam. The civil war.'

'Did you get proper care lately?'

'No. But I am getting it – right ... now!' exclaimed my cousin's joyous voice, removing beard and wig.

Bastard!

I shook with laughter. Ines goggled, quite literally.

'Why should you have a monopoly on fooling people, you sexy angel?'

They fell into each other's arms.

Discreetly wheeling out, I snatched a last croissant for the road. Why not?

XI

Happy endings aren't always happy beginnings. But when they last for three years, the famous itch nowadays – or so statistics posit – quite promising, right?

I have been privileged to be part of it. We travelled a lot together. Never dared I hope for such a loyal and caring friend as Ines. Never saw my cousin as happy. Never have I been so successful with my music and paintings – combined, we named them happenings. Things happened all the time anyway.

As kitschy as a sunset, one last detail: I now manage to walk with crutches.

Thomas dropped fashion shoots to do what he always wanted: enrol in film school. Ines started writing plays. Her panoramic imagination sprinkles her writing with wit. Upmost in her mind: avoid James-the-lawyer's muffled style at all costs.

Leading towards a situation without climax, as would a door leading nowhere ... and twice? No way. Keep it wry. Easy reading meant hard work.

On a postcard addressed to me, she scribbled: 'I boarded a plane. The woman next to me dropped her cardigan. I changed row. The End.'

Framed, it hangs above my pillow.

Though Ines's spoilt character has much improved, people don't change. At most, their behaviour does.

A month ago, they had a row. So what, you may ask?

By coincidence, it happened in Barcelona. Thomas rushed across the road in order to jump into a taxi. She ran after him and was hit by a car.

Other than haematomas and a fractured wrist, no visible injuries.